The Ruffler's Child

A Thomas the Falconer Mystery

John Pilkington

For Lisa and Nicky

Table of Contents

CHAPTER 1

Thomas had fed the merlin early that morning, but now, in the warm September afternoon, she was hungry again. She shook out her feathers ('rousing', falconers called it), standing proud on the thick gauntlet that covered his left hand and wrist, dark eyes alert, eager to fly at the quarry.

Up here on Greenhill Down there were larks in abundance - he had allowed her to kill several, and bagged them up to take back to Petbury. Sir Robert's cook would be glad of a delicacy to garnish tonight's supper. But this merlin, he knew, could take larger game. Thomas had never known one as spirited. Though tiny in comparison with the mighty birds - the soar hawks and goshawks with which Sir Robert and his friends delighted to hunt - she was nevertheless a princess among the smaller falcons. He believed she could fly at pigeons now, though they were as big as she; with more training she might take snipe, or even quail. He had raised her from a squeaky-voiced eyas, caught in July, and tended her through the long, dry summer with the patience and thoroughness for which Thomas Finbow the falconer was famous on the Berkshire Downs. He had plans for this little merlin: he would make a present of her to Lady Margaret. She would delight in the falcon as he did, choosing a fine name for her from a book, as was her custom. She would ride the Downs with the merlin on her embroidered gauntlet; she might even fashion a jewelled hood for her. Lady Margaret was a gentlewoman with a keen eye for fine things.

He frowned suddenly. Did his own desires dare to soar as high as falcons? He, a servant to her husband - he almost laughed at his foolishness. He decided he would let the merlin fly at a pigeon, if one appeared. As he stroked her folded wings with his forefinger, talking softly, she twitched suddenly and lifted a talon. Something had startled her. It startled Thomas too, for he had been alone on the hill for hours, expecting to see no one. He heard the noise: an odd sort of shuffling. He turned more quickly than he intended, unsettling the merlin, as something came noisily up the Ridgway below him. There was a shout from further down, and a man's running footsteps. The merlin flinched, jingling the tiny bells attached to her jesses, and Thomas fumbled in his pocket for the hood to quiet her.

Then he saw the bear.

A great brindled bear with a manged coat and a slobbering mouth, and a thick studded collar from which a chain swung wildly about, bounded up on all fours, snorting, and stopped barely ten yards away. Then it stood up on its hind legs, and peered at Thomas.

Thomas stood still as a rock, thinking only of the merlin, which was unnerved by the fearsome sight. Expertly he slipped the small hood over her head, clicking his tongue softly, murmuring in the gentle tones she understood. She quietened at once, as he tightened the jesses on her legs and gave the leash an extra turn about his arm. As he did so a man came hurrying uphill behind the bear, sweating and panting.

'He won't hurt thee,' the man said quickly, and caught hold of the end of the chain. As the bear turned towards him, the man pulled a bruised apple from his pocket and held it out. The bear's great jaws opened, and the apple was gone.

Thomas had been tense as a bent willow. He breathed out slowly in relief.

'I ask pardon if he frit thee,' the man said, in a thick northern accent.

He was recovering his breath. 'Ben don't run off, as a rule. Only, there's times he forgets hisself.'

He was a short, stocky man with a dark beard. His clothes were patched and stained from much travelling, though oddly, there was no pack on his back. Thomas nodded, and indicated the merlin.

'There's no harm done. She'll rest easy enough now.' He watched the bear, which still stood upright, munching the apple. 'It's rare indeed to see a bearward in these parts.'

The man shrugged and rubbed the bear's shaggy coat, saying: 'His name's Ben Stubbs. I took him out of London, away from the Bankside Pit. He were going blind. They'd have whipped him to death.' He grimaced. 'You ever seen that?'

Thomas shook his head. 'Heard about it. I'm not one for the bear-baiting.'

He saw now that the bear was indeed poor-sighted. It squinted vaguely in his direction, shaking its huge head.

The bearward watched the tall falconer with the soft grey eyes and russet beard, as he stroked the little falcon's back. Then he shifted on his feet, looking about him. He seemed eager all of a sudden to be gone.

'The road to Wantage. Am I in t' way of it?'

Thomas inclined his head towards the Ridgway. 'The path branches east, quarter of a mile on. Follow it downhill. You'll meet the road going north.'

The man jerked the bear's chain. It dropped on to all fours. 'I'm obliged to thee,' he said.

'Now I'd best find my road.'

As he moved forward, Thomas stepped back to let the two of them pass, but the bearward said: 'Old Ben wouldn't harm thee. He sees you're a friend to beasts.'

Then looking straight ahead, he started off at a fair pace.

Thomas watched man and bear trudge across the hill together, until striking the path they began to dip out of sight. Then he prepared to go his own way, in the opposite direction. He was thoughtful. Never before had he heard of a bearward using the old paths across the Downs. But then, since the harsh law against rogues and vagabonds was made more than a dozen years back, men like he had to shun the well-trodden routes. And there were many odd characters about the country nowadays. Migrant workers had been and gone, in this year of drought with its poor harvest - the twenty-ninth year of the reign of Queen Elizabeth.

His mind turning towards home, Thomas stooped to pick up the bag of larks and slung it over his shoulder. The merlin was quiet under her soft leather hood. He would leave the hood on for the journey down to Petbury.

Walking steadily, the bird on his fist, he came down off the Greenhill. After less than an hour the park, stables and kennels came into view, and beyond them Sir Robert Vicary's great house, lit by the sinking sun.

As he drew near to the falcons' mews, the lean-to which adjoined his cottage, he heard dogs barking and raised voices in the stable-yard. Thomas took the merlin back to her own perch, where she was kept apart from the larger falcons, placing a little food on the boards for her. He left the bells, varvels and jesses inside, made sure there was plenty of water for the birds, then walked over to the stables. As he rounded the yard wall he saw several people gathered round a nervous, sweating horse. Three dogs ran about excitedly, then bounded up to the falconer. He recognized the leash of hunting dogs belonging to Sir Robert's brother-in-law, the unpopular Nathaniel Pickering.

Nathaniel, Lady Margaret's older brother, had come to stay at Petbury last winter and become a part of the household. The gossip in the servants' hall was that he had squandered all his late father's money at the gambling tables or the trugging- houses, and was all but homeless. Thomas seldom listened to gossip, and did not like to pass judgement on a man, even one as surly as Nathaniel; but he had never been able to like him. Many times he had watched him riding home, the worse for drink, working the curb-rein on his horse so viciously that it bled from the mouth. He treated his dogs little better. Now they had gathered about Thomas' feet, tongues lolling. They were more than excited he thought - they were frightened. One of them had a gash on its cheek.

Martin, the house steward, called his name. Thomas walked across the yard where two stable-boys were trying to calm the high-spirited coursing-horse, which he now saw was indeed Nathaniel's. He began to understand the situation.

'They've come back without their master, then,' he said. Martin nodded, grim-faced. 'I would guess he's had a fall from the horse. But then, why didn't the dogs stay with him?'

'Perhaps he sent them back,' Thomas shrugged.

'Have you seen any sign on the Downs?'

Thomas shook his head. 'I saw a rare sight, though. A bear, with his keeper.'

Martin dismissed the matter. The grey, stooped old steward, a stickler for correctness, preferred to deal with one problem at a time. 'We'll have to mount a search. He could be grievously hurt.'

Thomas lowered his voice so that the stable-lads, who had managed to get the saddle off Nathaniel's horse, could not hear. 'Had he taken drink?'

Martin looked away. 'It's not my place to dwell on that, Thomas. Nor yours.'

Thomas sighed. 'We'd best fetch lanterns. It'll be dark in two hours.'

Martin was frowning. 'Sir Robert's gone to Reading on business. I don't like to assume the authority unless her ladyship allows.'

Thomas looked over the other's man's shoulder. 'She's here now.'

Lady Margaret Vicary, a cloak thrown over her indoor gown, was walking quickly towards them from the big house.

Martin turned respectfully towards her. The stable-lads stood awkwardly, trying to keep a firm hold on the anxious horse's bridle. But Lady Margaret swept past them, ignoring formalities.

'Do what must be done, Martin,' she said briskly. 'Take the gardeners and the beekeeper. Ask at South Wilby farm for more men if you need them. Tell them I would beg the favour.'

'Of course, my lady.' Martin hurried off, glad to have things clear at last. Thomas made as if to follow, but she checked him. 'I would speak a little with you.'

He stood in silence while she gave instructions to the boys to take good care of Nathaniel's horse and dogs. As they led the animals away, she drew close to Thomas.

She was as tall as he was (and as deep, some said). Her natural beauty and dignity, not to mention her city ways, stunned most of the simple Downland folk into silence. They sometimes wondered how Thomas seemed able to converse with her, almost as an equal. That she respected the quiet falconer above all the other servants, was common knowledge.

She spoke to him in the familiar tone she used when they were out hawking together.

'When you find my brother, whatever the circumstances, I would merely ask ...' she trailed off, watching a flock of crows flying overhead. Thomas waited.

'I would ask that you employ discretion.'

'A man may easily fall from his horse, madam,' Thomas said. 'There's no disgrace in an accident.'

'But we both know the likely reason he fell.'

Seeing her distress, he tried to speak reassuringly. 'I'd lay odds he's sitting up against a tree with nothing worse than a twisted ankle.'

A brief look of gratitude flickered across her face, though her speech remained brisk. 'Nathaniel took the south road when he rode out - that was barely an hour after dinner. He seldom rides further than the western edge of Lamboum Downs. Do you know where to begin looking?'

Thomas nodded. 'We'll find him, my lady. If it takes till dawn.'

Lady Margaret favoured him with a quick smile, then turned and walked back towards the house. Her step was as measured and graceful as usual. But to one who knew her she seemed preoccupied, beyond the mere likelihood of her brother's taking a tumble from his horse. After all, it would not be the first time the man had gone riding the worse for drink.

Dismissing the thought, Thomas walked back to his cottage.

When he lifted the latch and walked in, stooping under the oak lintel, Eleanor was settling a trencher on the table. She smiled with innocent pleasure and came quickly towards him. He bent to kiss her.

'I must go out, lambkin. I've no time for a real supper.'

Her eleven-year-old face clouded. He put down the bag of larks, and busied himself taking off gauntlet and jerkin. 'We're making a search for Master Nathaniel. Fell from his horse somewhere. I've come for the lantern.' He looked apologetic. 'You'll manage by yourself?'

She nodded. 'Mayhap I'll light the fire, sit with the mending, like mother used to. I can wait for you.'

He shook his head. 'I'll likely be out all night. When it grows dark, bar the door and get yourself to bed.'

She struggled to hide her disappointment. She liked nothing better than to sit up by firelight alone with her father, and talk until her eyes were closing. In the three years since Mary Finbow had died of the sweating sickness, it had become their habit. Eleanor liked to talk

about her mother; she seemed to find it comforting. For Thomas, there was still pain. Each year a little less perhaps, but the loss was with him every morning when he rose and she wasn't there beside him; then he went quickly out, as always, to tend to the falcons.

'If I'm not back by sunrise, you must feed the merlin and the two haggards,' he said, a shade distantly.

She knew his moods. She raised her face and gave a wan smile. At such times she was so like her mother, he had to look away.

'I got a bag of broken meat from the kitchen this afternoon,' she said.

He nodded towards the comer. 'There's some larks for supper, when you next see the cook.'

She went to cut some bread and a hunk of cheese while Thomas found the lantern and a tinder box. He took down a shepherd's cape from a peg. The clear skies had meant chilly nights this past week.

Silently Eleanor placed the bread and cheese on the table. He ate quickly, standing up as he often did, his thoughts elsewhere. After swallowing a few mouthfuls of water he was ready to leave. She opened the door for him and waited until he gave her the smile she expected.

'Goodnight, lambkin.'

As he stepped out, and she closed the door behind him, the sun was dipping behind the Downs. He made for the stable-yard, where a group of men with staves and lanterns had gathered, Martin the steward at their head. Without a word Thomas joined them, and the party set off at a steady walk, turning on to the south road. Petbury was soon lost behind them in the gathering gloom.

They had brought a bloodhound with them, and a worn shirt of Nathaniel's to give it a scent. For two hours the men tramped the lanes and meadows, searching the south side of Lambourn Downs as the dusk thickened and owls flew silently overhead. They saw nothing. When they first stopped to light the lanterns, there was little conversation. Now, grumbling began to break out.

'I hope he broke his neck,' the oldest of the gardeners said.

There was some snickering, but Martin rounded upon the man. 'I'll hear no more of that,' he said sternly. 'Whatever kind of a fellow he is, he's Master's brother-in-law and a gentleman.'

The path ahead of them bent slightly to the left. On the right was a small grove of beeches. Nightjars called in the distance. The bloodhound perked up suddenly, straining on his rope.

'Grimm's found a scent,' his handler said. Some of the men looked about, though there was nothing to be seen in the darkness. Beside the lane was a narrow ditch, but it was empty.

'Give him his head,' Thomas suggested. The handler untied the lead from the dog's collar. As the rope fell away, Grimm trotted forward, nose to the ground; then he broke into a run. The men followed, trying to keep up. They saw the dog turn abruptly to the right and leap over the ditch.

'He's making for the copse!' the handler shouted, his lantern swinging as he jumped the ditch. The others followed. The ground rose slightly as they moved towards the trees, the trunks of which gleamed in the lantern-light. The handler, in the lead with Thomas close behind him, called back over his shoulder: 'He's seen something!'

The men came straggling up, the fat beekeeper puffing in the rear. They slowed down as they saw Grimm halt on the edge of the beech grove. Whining, the dog backed away. His handler knelt beside him, murmuring 'What's matter, boy? Don't like the scent?'

Martin stepped forward into the trees, working his lantern from side to side. The others fanned out. They peered at the ground in all directions, but saw nothing untoward.

'Badger spooked 'im,' someone suggested. But the handler was uneasy. 'He's no fear of badgers. Something's wrong here.' Thomas walked slowly among the trees, his keen eyes scanning the ground. The grass had been disturbed. Then he saw a dark stain, and further on, at the base of a tree-trunk, an unnatural-looking mound, covered with grass and twigs.

'Over here,' he called, and started forward. At that moment Grimm the bloodhound howled, startling everybody.

The others found Thomas on his knees, uncovering a dark bulk. Suddenly he stiffened, and rose to his feet. The men of Petbury stood in a semi-circle, lanterns held high, staring in horror at the body of Nathaniel Pickering. He lay face upwards, eyes open, his mouth wrenched into what was almost a grin.

'My Good Lord,' the old gardener said, forgetting himself and making a sign of the cross, for he was of the old faith. But nobody paid him any attention. Their eyes roved downwards; Nathaniel's doublet and breeches were torn so badly, he was half-naked. And everywhere, the blood; his body was gashed, in some frenzied fashion, by knives or swords or heaven knew what, till it was merely a carcass. It looked a thing of evil.

For Thomas, it unlocked memories he kept hidden away in a part of his mind he rarely visited. Memories of a muddy field in the Low Countries, with the clash of pikes and the rattle of harquebuses and the screams of the wounded and dying ... when he went as a servant to old Sir Giles Vicary and found himself a mercenary soldier caught up in the killing of Spaniards. He a falconer, who was en route to Valkenswaard only to buy hawks for his master, had had a sword thrust into his hand, and been ordered to fight for his Queen or flee from the field like a coward. And he had fought, alongside his comrades from many corners of England who had come to help the Dutch rebels in their plight, and he had hacked and thrust like the others. He had seen men reduced to worse than beasts, slashing at corpses in their rage and bloodlust, leaving many a sight such as the one that lay before him. To come upon it in a peaceful English grove on a soft September night by the light of lanterns, sickened him. He pushed through the ring of men struck dumb in their shock, and stood apart, not wanting to see more.

CHAPTER 2

Sir Robert Vicary had come home late that same night, tired from his journey, and had barely gone to his bed when a servant woke him and Lady Margaret with the news. By early dawn, when the men brought Nathaniel's body back to Petbury and laid it in the small chapel, Sir Robert was in a poor temper which on this occasion he had to curb, if only out of feeling for Lady Margaret. Though he begged her to wait until her brother's corpse had been washed and dressed, she insisted on going to the chapel at once.

In the cold room lit by rush-lamps, Martin the steward sat near the body, which lay on a board across the altar. He had asked Thomas to keep vigil with him. They stood up in silence, as Sir Robert came in.

Their master was a big man, bulky in his fur-trimmed cloak., with thick brown hair and a narrow beard trimmed to a point. He stepped forward and looked down at Nathaniel, taking in the grim sight without a word. But Lady Margaret followed at almost a rim, flinging the door aside in her haste. Her gown fell half-open, causing the men to look away in embarrassment. She stopped abruptly, her face pale but set firm. She would not weep in front of them. Thomas lowered his eyes, realizing with a sudden jolt that he ached to take her in his arms and comfort her. He closed his fists, digging the nails into his palms until it hurt. This would not do.

The tension was broken unexpectedly by Lady Margaret's mousey-haired little servant Catherine, who came trotting in carrying a cloak, saying: 'My lady please, you must cover yourself!' Then seeing the blood-soaked body, she screamed in horror.

'Get her out!' Sir Robert shouted in fury. Martin hurried forward, glad of an excuse to be somewhere else. He pushed the terrified girl outside and followed, leaving only the master and mistress, and their falconer. Sir Robert took a deep breath and addressed Thomas quietly.

'Have you any notion how it happened?'

Thomas hesitated. An unpleasant theory had formed itself in his mind, on the long walk back to Petbury. He hated to voice it.

'There was a bear on the Downs yesterday, sir.'

'A bear?' Sir Robert's forehead creased in disbelief.

'With his keeper ... it got away from him, at least once. I saw them on the hill. He was making for Wantage, he said.'

'Would a bear do this to a man?' Sir Robert raised a hand and gestured helplessly.

'I don't know.' Thomas already regretted his words. The thought of the bearward being hauled in front of the magistrate and at the very least jailed, was bad enough. The thought of what fate would likely befall the bear that he clearly loved, was somehow worse.

'I don't believe it would.' Lady Margaret spoke, startling both men. Sir Robert put out a hand. She took it, though without enthusiasm.

'My dear, it does seem likely. There's no wild beast in England would tear a fellow like....' He broke off awkwardly. He was not a man of great tact. Rumour spoke of his being passed over for Lord Lieutenant of Berkshire, because in Court circles he was considered a bumpkin.

'I thought not of beasts,' his wife said. There are human devils abroad who would do it and laugh while they did it.'

Thomas was surprised at the violence of her retort. Sir Robert shook his head and turned back to the falconer.

'Had he a purse with him?'

Thomas nodded. 'Aye, untouched. And his dagger still in its sheath, and his cloak lying not far off. It was no robbery. Though,' he added as an afterthought, 'someone had dragged the body into a copse and tried to cover it with grass. A clumsy concealment.'

'Then we'll have this bear found,' Sir Robert snapped out, 'and its master too. I'll send to Lord Norreys for bailiffs. The man'll stand trial for his crime.'

'*His* crime?' Lady Margaret's voice was low. 'The bear's crime, surely.' Her body sagged, as if a string had snapped somewhere. Tears started in her eyes. She turned to leave, then spoke - not to her husband, but to Thomas.

'My brother was disliked, even hated here. I know that well enough.'

Thomas made no reply.

'He was a difficult man to love,' she added. Sir Robert made an attempt to place an arm about her, but to his consternation she shrugged him off. 'I tell you he wasn't always. He could have been a man of science, as our father was. There were things ...' she faltered, then finished lamely, 'matters of which all of you know nothing.'

The last remark was addressed to her husband. Then she shivered, and was gone through the doorway, eyes downcast. There was a brief silence in the chapel until Sir Robert, somewhat redfaced, turned to follow his wife outside. On an impulse Thomas spoke, surprising himself with his own boldness.

'Sir Robert.'

The knight stopped at the doorway. 'What is it?'

'May I have leave to examine him? The body, I mean.'

Sir Robert frowned. 'To what end?'

'I believe I - we may learn more of the matter.' He was aware the words sounded hollow, but Sir Robert nodded slowly.

'You have the best eye at Petbury. And some knowledge of corpses, I allow.'

Thomas disliked the edge to the voice, but nodded in return. 'I was a soldier, sir. Albeit briefly.'

'Well, look all you want,' Sir Robert said. 'The crones will come by shortly to wash him.' He snorted suddenly. 'By the time he's cased for burial he'll look better than he has for years.'

Later that morning, having spoken to Eleanor and tended to the falcons, Thomas returned to the chapel where two old women with experience of such tasks were washing Nathaniel Pickering's body. When Thomas informed them that he had his master's permission to examine it the women were disgusted, and told him plainly that his actions were devilish, if not blasphemous. Ignoring their complaints, he rolled his sleeves back and steeled himself to the grisly task. Soon enough, his pains were rewarded.

Once the blood had been washed away, the gashes on the body were found to be quite shallow. They were parallel, and resembled only too clearly the claw-marks of a large animal. Most ran diagonally across the chest and shoulders, but there were other cuts in several directions on the belly and thighs. It looked as though the bear - for the bear it must be, Thomas concluded with a sinking heart - had clawed its victim as he lay on the ground.

The evidence seemed plain enough. Lady Margaret's brother, at a little over forty years of age, had died a ghastly death. The bear had probably reared up suddenly from the roadside startling the horse, which could easily have thrown its rider, especially one unsteady from drink. As he staggered to his feet it could have attacked him, perhaps enraged by his shouts - Nathaniel was a noted ranter and curser. This might explain why the horse, and the dogs too, had run away, no doubt terrified of the onslaught by such a huge, unfamiliar creature. One question arose, however: what was the bearward doing, during all of this time?

When the women turned the body over Thomas found no claw-marks on its back, but there was blood there, too. Had Nathaniel writhed about on the ground, struggling to ward off his attacker? But now, other questions began to surface in Thomas's mind, the principal one being: how exactly had Nathaniel Pickering died?

His throat was not touched, nor his heart, nor any vital organ that Thomas could see. The

gashes, though they had caused much bleeding, were superficial. Perhaps, he reasoned, the

man had died of shock - suffered a seizure of some kind. Thomas had not the medical knowledge to look for such signs; perhaps a surgeon should be sent for.

Then, as the washing-women wiped the blood from Nathaniel's back, he saw the hole.

It was small, so that he almost missed it. But peering close, while the other two clicked their tongues in disgust, he pressed down the skin at the centre of the spine and saw it part to reveal a circular opening. Pressing harder, he saw that the wound went deep into the back, perhaps severing the spinal cord. A wound like that could have killed him - and it was not made by any bear.

'What now, falconer?' one of the women asked, but Thomas did not reply. His mind was busy. This was no dagger-wound; nor would a sword have made such a shape - in any case, the middle of the back was no place for a sword-thrust. Then, he saw the answer was obvious. Nathaniel had been shot by a crossbow.

Whoever did it was a good marksman. He had found his target, and he had retrieved the bolt - the edges of the wound were torn where it had been pulled out.

The elation Thomas had at first felt, now ebbed away quickly. The implications of this were grave indeed. But, wasn't he forgetting the claw-marks? Had the bear found the man dead by the roadside and mauled him - or worse, had it found him dying, and finished the business?

Thomas straightened up, aware that his first task was to inform Sir Robert. He was aware, too, of the distress this would cause Lady Margaret. The women had stopped work and were looking at him.

'You can finish the washing, and dress him too,' Thomas said. 'But there's more to this than I thought. It's a matter of murder.'

Both of them inhaled sharply; one clasped a hand to her mouth. Without further word, Thomas left the chapel and went outside to wash his hands. It was good to be in the open, with the breeze in his face, but fatigue descended on him; he had had no sleep. With a heavy heart, he started towards the great house.

Events unfolded quickly that day. The Lord Lieutenant's men caught the bearward - not in the vicinity of Wantage, but on the road to Didcot several miles away. He claimed to know nothing of Nathaniel Pickering, nor anyone else. Instead of taking him to Reading gaol, the men were ordered to bring him first to Petbury. The coroner's inquest would be held there, near to the place where the deceased had met his end. Village men would be sworn in as a jury. Meanwhile Nathaniel Pickering's body, cleaned and dressed in his best clothes, lay in his black-draped coffin, with bunches of yew and rosemary tied to it.

Sir Robert was exasperated by the whole business. It was no secret that he had loathed his brother-in-law as much as anyone else, and only gave him a roof because Lady Margaret wished it. Had Nathaniel died after a drunken fall from his horse - or even from a mauling by a half-crazed bear - he would have been more than satisfied to give him a Christian burial in the family sepulchre, issue instructions about the proper period of mourning, then return to normality as quickly as possible. The revelation that he had been murdered upset everything. And at first, Sir Robert felt inclined to blame Thomas.

'How can you be certain?' he grumbled, pacing about in the wide hall at Petbury the following afternoon, his shoes scuffing on the rush-strewn floor.

Thomas stood before him, his mouth set firm. 'I've seen men killed by crossbow, sir,' he said for the third time. 'Whoever did it, knew his business. An ex-soldier, surely.'

'But why!' Sir Robert thundered. 'God knows Nathaniel was not well-liked, but what had anyone to gain by killing him?'

Martin the steward, long accustomed to his master's ways, stood in silence near Lady Margaret, who sat dressed in black beside the huge mahogany table. While her face bore no expression, it was clear that she was shaken by the events.

'Thomas is merely the discoverer of the deed,' she said finally. 'He is not a conjurer. Might he be allowed to return to his duties?'

Sir Robert glowered into the wide fireplace, in which a huge fire burned. Outside, the weather had turned at last; rain drove against the casements. At last he aimed a curt nod at the falconer. 'You did well to find it out,' he said. 'Though I wish with all my heart you hadn't.'

'As I do, sir,' Thomas said, though inwardly aware how glad he was that the bear was not to blame.

But as if he had read his thoughts, Sir Robert said abruptly: 'We still need to discover why Nathaniel's body came to be torn half to pieces.'

At that moment the door opened, and the Vicary children came in. William, now turned sixteen and soon to go off to the University, was a handsome youth with long, fair hair and a sensitive face. He had of late become something of a dandy; the sleeves of his doublet were slashed to show yellow silk beneath. Behind him, walking with small, delicate steps in her long black gown, came his sister Anne, two years younger, her face bearing evidence of some displeasure.

'What is the matter?' Sir Robert was nettled at the interruption. Anne went to her father, who despite his temper would deny her nothing, and William to the mother he resembled so closely.

'Why aren't you at your lessons?' Lady Margaret asked her son.

William tossed his head. 'How can I study, with Uncle Nat's death suffusing the house like a bad odour?' He glared at Anne. 'And a sister whose sole pleasure in life is to torment me!'

Anne's eyes filled with tears, she appealed to her father. 'I am the one who's tormented! He mocked my French accent - he said I hadn't the wit of a scullery-maid!'

Sir Robert turned swiftly on William, but Lady Margaret moved wearily to avert the blast.

'The death is a shock to us all,' she said. 'Not least to me, William. I have lost my brother.'

The youth lowered his eyes.

'Quiet restraint is the correct mode of behaviour, with a funeral hard upon us,' Lady Margaret continued, including her daughter in the statement. 'To be followed by a proper period of mourning. I had thought each of you old enough by now to show tolerance.'

Anne's lower lip trembled. Clumsily, her father bent and kissed his daughter quickly on the forehead. 'Your mother is correct,' he murmured. 'In any case you should not interrupt your brother when he is studying. But perhaps...' He glanced at his wife. 'Perhaps studies might be suspended, until after the burial?'

Lady Margaret gave a nod. 'I think that would be wise.'

A thin, gangling young man in a grey threadbare suit and gown came nervously into the room. John Pollard, an Oxford scholar, was William's tutor. It was also known that he wrote love-poetry, though he neither showed nor read it to anyone save William; he and his charge were close. Sir Robert thought there was something distasteful about their friendship, especially when he saw them sniggering together over some book or other. Now he turned testily upon the tutor, who stood near the door scratching his cheek as he was apt to do at moments of tension.

'There'll be no more lessons until after the funeral, Master Pollard,' Sir Robert said. 'You can take yourself off somewhere and scribble.'

Pollard winced, but stood his ground. 'I'm most grateful, Sir Robert. But I thought it prudent to inform you that there is a body of men outside, with a large bear.'

There were mixed reactions in the hall. William and Anne, their feud forgotten, ran to the windows and looked out, as curious as children of any age. Thomas and Martin exchanged glances.

Lady Margaret rose to her feet, saying to her husband: 'I will leave you to deal with the matter.' To her daughter she said: 'That animal is not a fit object for your curiosity. Come with me.'

Martin and Thomas bowed as she went out, Anne following. Pollard darted aside to let her pass. Sir Robert, Martin and Thomas went to the window, and looked out upon a sobering sight: the bearward, hands tied behind his back, standing in the courtyard between two burly sheriff's men armed with staves. Several other men held the bear, by a series of taut ropes raying outwards as from a maypole, so that no man was within reach of the creature's claws. Not that it seemed likely to threaten any of them, Thomas thought, with a deal of pity. The animal hung its head wearily, as did its keeper, the two of them standing in the rain, the very picture of dejection.

Sir Robert issued instructions to his steward. 'Have the bear locked up securely, and tethered. The fellow....' He thought for a moment. Petbury was a manor, not a castle; there was no lock-up here. Thomas took the opportunity to speak.

'Might man and bear be kept together, sir? The creature may grow troublesome without his master. We could put them in the old malt-house. There's no window, and a strong enough door.'

Sir Robert nodded in satisfaction. 'Very well. We'll keep them there until the coroner arrives.'

Looking out at the bear and his ward standing on the wet cobbles, the knight's pinched face softened slightly. He turned from the window. William, who had been unable to take his eyes from the curious sight, asked: 'What'll become of them, Father?'

Sir Robert walked away and stood with his back to the fire. 'This morning, I would happily have seen the fellow hang,' he said. 'But he is no murderer, I'll venture that much. Unless he has a passport signed by two justices, which I doubt, he'll be whipped and branded as a vagrant. But from that, a man can recover. As for the beast ...' he shrugged. Nobody spoke. It was plain enough: whatever the coroner's jury decided, the bear would be put to death.

And one matter still remained unresolved. Somewhere, the murderer of Nathaniel Pickering was still at large.

CHAPTER 3

In this year of 1586, with rumours the length and breadth of England about popish plots to assassinate the Queen, the most exciting event on the Downs, indeed the only event talked of, was the coroner's inquest at Petbury. Villagers crammed the black-draped banqueting hall; it was the first time most of them had been inside Sir Robert's grand house. Sixteen of them, mainly shopkeepers and craftsmen, were sworn in as jurors. They sat in hushed anticipation as Sir Robert and Lady Margaret entered accompanied by the acting coroner, Sir William Stanton, one of Sir Robert's hunting friends. Martin the steward was recognized, along with others from the estate as they took their places. Some pointed out Thomas Finbow the falconer as the man who had found the body of Lady Margaret's ill-favoured brother. Few had anything good to say of the deceased, but it had been a grisly death, and folk were inclined to be charitable. There was suppressed excitement as Sir William called for silence and opened the proceedings.

Martin, Thomas and other men from the search party told how they had discovered the body. Thomas gave further testimony of how he had found the wound. Old Doctor Scambler was called, and reported in a barely audible muttering how he had examined the deceased, and confirmed Thomas's findings as the most likely cause of death. Then excitement swelled, as the coroner ordered the bearward to be brought in.

He walked stiffly through the hall, a stocky man with a dark beard, his face set hard. There was silence as he took the oath and began to answer in a broad Yorkshire accent. Thomas, close by, could not help but pity the man.

He gave his name as Edward Mace. He was born in Leeds but had left there long since, to seek work in London. He had a way with beasts, and had worked at the Bankside arenas, the bull and bear pits in Southwark, but the work began to sicken him. During the summer he often wandered the land, taking bears to show, sometimes as part of a juggling troupe, sometimes alone. He liked the life; he had no regrets. He swore that none of his bears had ever harmed a living soul, not even the half-blind one, Ben Stubbs. This bear was not born in England, he admitted: he thought it came from Muscovy, on a ship. Tension rose in the hall, as Sir William now came to the matter of the death of Nathaniel Pickering. For a moment, it looked as if Mace was about to deny everything, as he had consistently done to the sheriff's men. But now he looked about the room, his gaze settling on the face of Thomas the falconer.

There was a short silence, before he faced the coroner and said:

'We found him, on t' roadside. His horse were close by, and his dogs. I swear to thee, master - he were already dead.'

Talk broke out at once, causing Sir William to rap irritably on the table. He gestured to Mace to continue.

'He were lying on his front. As I come up, dogs went wild. That's what set Ben off, the dogs. Bad memories for him, see.'

A murmur began to rise, and Sir William called again for silence. Beside him, Sir Robert's forehead was creasing into the familiar frown. Only Lady Margaret seemed unmoved, sitting motionless to one side in her mourning gown. The coroner pressed his enquiry. 'What happened then?'

'He broke from me, Ben did. Mauled the fellow - I tried to stop him, but it were t' scent of dogs as did it. He turned t' body and slashed it bad, 'fore I could get hold of him and settle him. He's not mazed like that as a rule, I swear to thee he's not.'

'How can you be certain he was dead?' Sir William's voice was harsh. It was clear he had little sympathy for the man. But Mace was eager to speak now.

'I saw him, when Ben turned him over. His eyes were open - he were limp as a rag. I thought he'd fallen from t' horse and snapped his neck, or his back. But I've not the knowledge.'

'What did you do?' Sir William asked.

'After I got Ben settled, I slapped the horse on t' rump and sent it away. Dogs ran after it. They were scared of Ben, more after he cuffed one of 'em on t' cheek. They weren't fighting dogs.'

Thomas was relieved to hear that the testimony of Edward Mace bore the stamp of truth. It fitted with his own observations: of the nervous horse and dogs, one with the cut on its face, and of the state of the body.

'If you speak truly,' Sir William asked blandly, 'why then did you not report your finding? Why not summon assistance?'

Mace levelled a frank gaze at him. 'Who'd have believed me? An outsider, and a vagabond to boot - would thee?'

After a moment Sir William said: 'Finish your testimony.'

The bearward shrugged. 'I have, all but. I dragged him off t' road into some trees and covered him. There were no one about. I left him there and cut across Downs. Ben were out of sorts, so I meant to tire him out a bit, on t' hills.'

He pointed suddenly to Thomas. 'I saw yon falconer, with his bird. He'll tell thee.'

Sir William's gaze flickered briefly towards Thomas, who was nodding. There was a muttered exchange at the top table, then Sir Robert

31

asked: 'Have you ever been a soldier?

''No, sir,' Mace answered.

'Can you handle a crossbow?'

The man shook his head. 'I've no skill wi' weapons, save a cudgel.'

'Did you see anyone else on the road, earlier that day?'

It was Sir William who had spoken. At this, Mace hesitated. 'There were some folk on t' way to Reading, I recall, and some t' other direction, for Swindon.'

'On horseback, or on foot? What sort were they?'

Mace shrugged. He seemed uneasy. Then an old man from the village stood up suddenly, and called out: 'I was on the road that day, sir. I saw a band of men.'

There was a stir in the hall 'You have not been called,' Sir William answered testily. Then he asked: 'What sort of men?'

'Vagrom men, sir,' the man answered. 'Masterless folk, on foot. One was an Abram man in a yellow coat, one o' they as feigns madness to get charity. Laughing all the time, only 'twas but play-acting.'

There was considerable interest in the hall at this news. Such people were known well enough. Some masterless men were genuinely seeking employment, others had darker aims. An Abraham man had come begging last spring, his skin burned horribly with spearwort to arouse sympathy. Martin the steward had seen through the ruse, and sent the man about his business.

Sir William turned back to Edward Mace. 'Did you not see these men?' he asked.

Mace shook his head firmly. 'No, sir. Never saw 'em.'

'Have you anything more to tell us?' Sir William asked, peering intently at him.

Mace shook his head again, then said: 'Ben Stubbs didn't kill no one, sir. I ask mercy - not for me, for Ben.'

Sir William fixed him with a grim look. 'It's for the jury to decide,' he said. 'But whatever their verdict, a beast such as yours cannot be allowed to walk freely about the land.'

He nodded to the bailiff who stood at Mace's shoulder. Mace was led out of the room. As he went, his eyes met those of Thomas the falconer, then dropped quickly.

There were no other testimonies. The jury huddled in a comer to deliberate, but there was

little surprise when after less than an hour they delivered their verdict. Nathaniel Pickering had been unlawfully killed, shot through the back by a person or persons unknown. The bear, they added, overstepping themselves in their enthusiasm for the task, ought to be put to death at once by burning, and his owner forced to witness the event as a lesson.

Sir William issued an appeal for any man with knowledge of Nathaniel Pickering's death to come forward, but it was clear the business was over. Thomas rose from his seat, an emptiness inside him. He walked out of the house and made for the falcons' mews. He wanted to be away from people and their cruelty, up on the Downs with a hawk on his hand, and watch it soar high into the air, free as the clouds, taking his cares with it.

Nathaniel's funeral took place the next day, the body being taken from the house, where it had laid in the intervening days, to the chapel. Forty mourners from the village, paid a shilling each by Sir Robert and clothed in black drugget at his expense, walked solemnly behind the coffin on its horse-litter, a rich canopy held above it. Some of the mourners carried branches of bay or yew. The family followed, cloaked in black and carrying garlands; Sir Robert and Lady Margaret first, with William and Anne behind. There were no other relatives present, save a cousin of Sir Robert's who had barely known the deceased. Lady Margaret, it was well known, had no other family beside her late brother.

Members of the Petbury household completed the pageant: John Pollard, stiff and awkward in a suit of black; Martin the steward with his staff of office. Behind came the host of servants who made up the retinue of a wealthy knight of the realm like Sir Robert Vicary: the kitchen-maids and cooks and washerwomen, the serving-men and grooms and farm-workers in their fustian, and towards the rear, taller than most, Thomas the falconer with his daughter Eleanor, a black cloak over her woollen dress.

The ceremony was a rather tense affair, for clouds scudded in from the west, bringing a threat of rain. Stuffy Doctor Wickes intoned the burial service, flowers and branches of evergreen were cast on the coffin, and two songs of lamentation were sung. Some village women then broke into ritual weeping, transparently false in view of the kind of man the deceased was. When it was finally over, Sir Robert - with obvious relief - led the procession back to the house, where everyone looked forward to the funeral feast with some relish. Sir Robert had his faults, but meanness on such occasions was not one of them.

During the festivities - for such they quickly became, now that Nathaniel was laid to rest – Thomas sat near the doorway, while ale, bread and cakes vanished rapidly from the long tables. Lady Margaret had retired to her chamber. Sir Robert, after a token appearance, had excused himself, to everyone's satisfaction, and now the wake took on the cheerful aspect of a wedding, as drink flowed and the gossip grew more uninhibited. It was wrong to speak ill of the dead, folk murmured, then told tales of Nathaniel Pickering's surliness and selfishness. A young maid wondered why he had never married, prompting knowing looks from men who sat near. Perhaps no woman would have him, the cook said, whereupon one of the stable- lads blurted out that the boot was on the other foot: more like - he wanted no woman.

There was a hush then, and people looked away. Thomas had heard the whispers: there were those who thought Nathaniel Pickering guilty of what Doctor Wickes referred to in his sermons as 'the abominable vice,' still punishable by death, though this was almost never enforced. For his part, Thomas had little interest in the man. Generally, he had managed to keep his distance from him, since Nathaniel rarely hunted with hawks; in fact, he and Lady Margaret had spent little time together. Thomas had occasionally wondered at their lack of affection for each other; though it was true Nathaniel was not a man to inspire such feelings in anyone, even a younger sister.

Thomas drained his mug, thinking of the falcons. The birds needed exercise, after the disruption of the past few days. He stood up, made his brief farewells and walked out into the wide flagged passage. There he saw John Pollard standing outside the door, leaning against the wall. He was pale and gangling as ever, but never before had Thomas seen him weep. Tears ran down his cheeks and on to his wrinkled collar.

'Master Pollard?' Thomas was unsure whether or not he wanted to be left alone, but to his surprise Pollard looked sharply at him and said: 'There is a God of vengeance, and he has done his work!'

He stepped forwards, eyes wide. He is not used to drink, Thomas thought, but the tutor's speech was coherent enough as he said: 'The man was a devil, and now he's dead, but the harm he did may still haunt the living!'

'What do you speak of?' Thomas asked. Pollard put out an unsteady hand and to Thomas's discomfort, took him by the collar. 'My charge is away to Oxford, and I'm to be cast out soon. No longer wanted - so I care not a jot what I say, falconer.' As he leaned closer, Thomas smelled the beer on his breath.

'He owned knowledge, that is power. *Scientia est potentia,* falconer. And he was brutal in its application.'

'Tell me outside,' Thomas said, some instinct telling him that this was perhaps a matter of importance. But the tutor let his hand fall away. He wiped his eyes with a sleeve, like a miserable schoolboy, and sniffed loudly.

'No matter ... he can't hurt me anymore,' he muttered. 'No man can; save one.' He broke off and moved towards the staircase.

Loud voices and laughter came from the hall behind them. Thomas made as if to stop Pollard, but a kitchen-maid hurried by at that moment, pushing between them. As the tutor reached the stairs a door opened somewhere above. Pollard looked up, as did Thomas, to see the face of William Vicary peering over the balusters.

Pollard stood with his hand on the newel-post, staring upwards, as an odd smile spread over William's delicate features. Then with a casual wave of his hand he turned and disappeared. A door banged shut.

Instead of going upstairs, Pollard sat down heavily on the bottom step, and gave himself up to a pitiful, childlike outpouring of grief. Without a word, Thomas left him alone.

A week later, in the early days of October, a hawking party set out on the Downs for the first time since before Nathaniel's death.

It was a fresh, sunny morning with a clear scent of autumn, and the group rode across the open hilltops scattering flocks of sheep, each man and woman with a bird on the fist. Sir Robert carried a fine soar hawk, a tercel named Glory. Sir Marcus Brooke, his guest for the day, bore a great passage-hawk named Caesar. Sir Marcus was the wealthiest landowner in this part of the county, a man with a fine town house in London, and connections at Court. His wife, Lady Alice, had a small lanner falcon on her gauntlet, while Lady Margaret, to Thomas's quiet satisfaction, now carried the little merlin. She had named the bird Melisande, she told Thomas, after the daughter of a king of Jerusalem.

Thomas rode a gelding from the Petbury stable. He carried no hawk himself, but was to oversee the day's sport. Grooms and men from the estate would follow later with the short-winged falcons, the sparrowhawks and Sir Robert's favourite, a mighty goshawk named Speed. Other men would run ahead with setter dogs to flush out the game. It was fine hawking weather, without too much wind, and Sir Robert planned to hunt first at 'high mountee' in the open country, taking partridges and quails, and perhaps a bittern or heron; he and Sir Marcus had a small wager on the relative skills of their birds. After two or three hours the party would move southwards off the hills into the wooded parts of the Lambourn Valley, for the 'flight at brook,' which was equally popular. There the short-winged hawks would be brought up to fly at ducks and pheasants for the pot. Sir Robert was eager for a good day's

hunt followed by a grand supper - partly to cheer his wife, who was still in mourning. Today, however, she appeared to have more of a sparkle in her eye. She had been especially touched when her falconer presented her with the little merlin, in a new hood which his daughter had embroidered.

'Eleanor shall have a gold sovereign on her birthday,' Lady Margaret said.

'Very kind, my lady,' Thomas answered, riding beside her. He had seen little of the mistress in the past few days. After all the excitement, things were returning to normal. Nothing more was said of Nathaniel's death: there seemed to be a tacit acceptance that whoever his murderer was, he would probably never be found.

Edward Mace had been taken off to Reading gaol; neither he nor his bear was expected to be seen again. There had been other departures, too: the Michaelmas term had begun at Oxford University and William Vicary was gone to Oriel College, where his father had been an unwilling and undistinguished scholar. John Pollard, his employment as tutor ended, had departed for London. Thomas did not see him again after the funeral festivities, but he had not forgotten. In fact, his mind dwelt more on the events of the past weeks than he liked. He had a feeling that things were not right - particularly with regard to Lady Margaret. He could not but feel that she seemed oddly unconcerned about discovering who had killed her brother.

This morning, while the falcons soared and stooped at their quarry, and the watchers shouted their approval, Lady Margaret remained silent. Lady Alice, loud-voiced and more than a dozen years her senior, barely noticed, riding with the men and urging her own bird to fly at partridges. But the lanner was too small and when, finally, she took a pigeon, to Lady Alice's disgust the bird carried off to a distant tree and sat perched at the top, out of reach. The men guffawed, but Lady Margaret, seen by nobody save Thomas, rode a little apart and sat on her horse, looking away. To his surprise, she half-turned in the saddle and gestured to him to join her.

Thomas rode up and drew his mount to a halt beside her. When she turned her face he half-expected her to be weeping, thinking perhaps of her brother. But she appeared calm and addressed him quietly as always.

*

'I have a commission for you, Thomas.'

He waited, sitting his horse in the mild sunshine, while the shouts of the hawkers rang in the distance. Lady Margaret turned her chestnut mare about to face him, then patted the animal's well-groomed neck. Her other arm remained raised, with the merlin perched docilely upon her clenched hand.

'I shall go to London soon, and I want you to accompany me.'

When he registered surprise, she went on quickly: 'Sir Marcus has heard of some fine gyrfalcons, shipped from Norway. A rare prize, you will agree.'

He nodded.

'Sir Robert and I discussed the matter at breakfast. He has business to attend to here - but in any case, you have the better eye. You must purchase a falcon for him. For my part, I have business of my own; I wish to tidy up my brother's affairs. My late father's house has been sold, but we hear it remains empty. Nobody knows why. Nor, for that matter, who the purchaser is.'

She was thoughtful for a moment. 'I have a mind to see it, perhaps for the last time.'

'What of my daughter, Lady Margaret?' Thomas asked.

'You need have no concerns,' she answered. 'She shall take her meals in the house, and sleep there too if you wish. She may have Catherine's bed, since Catherine will, of course, come with me.' She considered a moment. 'It's time we found regular employment for Eleanor in any case. She's hardly a child any more, is she?'

'I suppose not, my lady,' Thomas muttered absently. He had the feeling that he was not going to London merely to purchase an expensive falcon for his master. With a trace of amusement, Lady Margaret asked suddenly: 'What is the matter? You look frightened.'

'No, my lady,' Thomas answered, then added: 'I merely... I've not been to London much - not for some years. I have no knowledge of the city.'

'Never fear,' Lady Margaret said, with no discernible trace of sarcasm. 'If necessary I will hold your hand.'

At that, he recovered himself. 'No need for that, my lady,' he said stiffly. 'As long as I have instruction as to where the hawks are to be had. I can strike a bargain as well as anyone.'

'If I doubted your proficiency,' Lady Margaret said, 'I should not have suggested for one moment that you accompany me.'

'You suggested it?' Thomas asked, and regretted it at once.

At that moment the little merlin mantled on the gauntlet, spreading her wings impatiently.

Lady Margaret clicked her tongue with affection.

'Melisande is eager for the chase. Or perhaps, merely hungry.'

She paused, then said deliberately: 'One who has fed only on scraps may pine for a change

of diet.'

His heart gave a jolt. There was a directness in her gaze, that left him bereft of speech.

'My lady..." he began, feeling the blood rise to his face, but Lady Margaret, gripping the rein in her gloved hand, was urging her horse forward. 'Sir Robert will speak to you about the gyrfalcon,' she said. 'Now, shall we rejoin the hunt?'

And before he could touch his boot-heels to his own mount, she was riding smartly away towards the rest of the party. As she did so, the black mourning-ribbons fluttered from her tall riding-hat and fell to the ground. Thomas was about to stop and recover them; but for some reason he thought better of it, and rode after his mistress.

CHAPTER 4

It was settled that Lady Margaret, accompanied by Thomas and her maid Catherine, would leave for London the following Monday, breaking their journey at Windsor. Sir Marcus Brooke had generously offered the use of his town house, near the Temple. He and Lady Alice would not be there, but Lady Margaret was free to stay as long as she wished; the housekeeper had been informed.

Rumours were rife at Petbury: Nathaniel had left a pile of debts, and his old house had been sold to pay them; Lady Margaret was taking Thomas with her as a bodyguard, in case she was waylaid by creditors. The fact that Sir Robert was not accompanying his wife prompted less gossip: it was known that he disliked London, and was seldom seen at Court.

In the chilly dawn, Thomas said goodbye to Eleanor at the cottage door, reminding her to keep a close eye on the falcons. One of the grooms was to have charge of the birds in his absence. The man was competent enough, yet still Thomas was anxious. He told her once again to check the hut morning and night.

'All will be well, Father,' Eleanor said, shivering a little in her cloak. 'I shall easily get scraps now I am to help in the kitchen.' She brightened suddenly. 'You will bring me a gift from London?'

He nodded and kissed her, then shouldered his pack and walked to the stable-yard where mounts were being readied. Now that the time had come, he felt a deep pang of regret. His heart was here, on the Berkshire Downs; he hated to leave.

At the stables, he waited as the party emerged from the house: Lady Margaret in her fine riding-clothes, accompanied by Sir Robert and Martin, with Catherine close behind her mistress. Grooms led the horses forward, and Sir Robert helped his wife into the saddle. Catherine, half-nervous, half-excited, said:

'Imagine me in London town, Thomas - I never been further than Newbury!'

When all were mounted, Sir Robert moved close to Thomas and said: 'I'm entrusting my wife's safety to you, falconer.'

'I know that well, sir,' Thomas said.

'When you get to the house in Sything Lane tomorrow, the lawyer will meet you. His name, I am told, is Nicholas Stocker. Trust no one else, you understand?'

'Yes, Sir Robert,' Thomas replied.

'It's no more than seventy miles, husband,' Lady Margaret said. 'We're not taking ship for the Indies.'

'Even so,' Sir Robert insisted, 'I ask you to take care.' Then he added: 'That gyrfalcon - I want the finest of the batch, remember. No matter what it costs me!'

Standing beside Martin, who was lugubrious as usual in the grey morning, Sir Robert managed a smile and raised his hand, as the party clattered off the cobbles and rode down the lane towards the wide gates of Petbury. In a matter of minutes the house was hidden from view, as they turned on to the road running south from Wantage. After a further two miles, they reached the great highway that led to Reading and beyond; the road to London.

The journey was pleasant enough, though Lady Margaret barely spoke to her two companions until they reached Windsor that evening, saddle-sore and weary, and put up at a large inn. Thomas saw that the mounts were fed and cared for, while Catherine attended to the accommodation she and her mistress would share. Lady Margaret retired early, taking supper in her room. Thomas, having eaten and taken a mug with the men gathered round the tap-room fire, went early to his own bed. As he was drifting off to sleep, he heard the rain begin to fall.

By morning, the road was a quagmire.

Despite their cloaks and hoods, the three riders were quickly soaked to the skin and dispirited, so that they took little notice of the villages en route: Uxbridge, Hillingdon, Brentford - all were glimpsed dimly through the downpour until at last, as they rode through Shepherd's Bush late on the Saturday afternoon, the rain stopped, and a pale sun slid out from behind ragged, hurrying clouds.

Passing Tyburn gibbet, which was empty but looked sinister enough at the best of times, they were soon at St-Giles-in-the-Fields, whence it was but a short ride down Holborn, through Lincoln's Inn and across the Fleet Ditch by Holborn Bridge, a right turn down Snow Hill before West Smithfield with the crowds growing thicker all the time, and thence through the city walls via Newgate - and suddenly, they were in London.

Sything Lane, where Lady Margaret's old family house stood, was at the eastern end of the city close to Great Tower Hill, which necessitated a difficult journey the entire length of London. Since Thomas was unsure of the route, Lady Margaret led the way, while he and Catherine rode close behind her through the dirt and noise of the streets. The throng was about them now like a flood; all the panorama of raw humanity that made up the great, roaring capital which had grown, it was said, to almost two hundred thousand souls. To a simple country girl like poor Catherine, it was a nightmare. She kept her small pony pressed close up against Thomas's big sorrel horse and tried to look straight ahead, ignoring the shouts and cries and strange accents that assailed her senses from every side.

Here in Newgate Market were the alewives and fruit-sellers and costermongers, the poulterers and butchers in the Shambles past Stinking Lane, the rowdy prentice-boys and the fat beadles and the trulls in their red taffeta gowns going into St Paul's to do business. Here were disapproving Puritans in simple black suits, clashing with loud-voiced young gentlemen in garish doublets of sarsenet and satin, swords swinging at their sides. In West Cheap, rich merchants' wives in gowns and periwigs swept in and out of the shops on Goldsmiths' Row, and there was the carriage of some lord or lady, rich beyond the dreams of poor folk who pressed about it on all sides, so that the red-faced coachman flailed his whip and shouted to clear the way.

By Ironmongers Lane, councillors in sober clothes crossed to the Guildhall in Basinghall Street, and the crowds thickened again, coming fast from the Poultry and down from Cornhill, as Lady Margaret veered her horse to the right into Lombard Street. Through the press of Gracious Street, another market, they forced a passage, with the ballad-singers singing their wares, and from every side the church bells beginning to strike five o'clock, outdoing each other in their cacophony. Here the crowd was at its thickest, for to the right was Fish Street Hill and the great thoroughfare down to London Bridge, the only way across the river save by boat. The stench of the Thames seemed discernible even from this distance, as they bore left into Little Eastcheap. And here, were the beggars

There had been a sprinkling of them all along the way, especially at the markets, but here they congregated in a line, as if by some prior

45

arrangement. Lady Margaret ignored them, as did Catherine, though her nervousness was such that some laughed at the little country maid, tossing lewd remarks and invitations at her as she passed. Thomas dropped back beside her and looked hard upon the nearest of the men to show that the girl had his protection. But in his heart, he had not the will to condemn them, for they were a pitiful sight.

They were of all kinds, of all ages and both sexes. Many were merely poor folk from various parts of the city and beyond, some with ragged children at their sides, asking for the price of a loaf. Others were sick or disabled, with their missing limbs and their sores, crying desperately for charity. But among them were the professional beggars, actors every one, each with a part to play. Palliards stood in patched clothes, some with a 'kinchin mort' - a beggar's child - at their sides, to increase sympathy. A 'counterfeit crank,' foaming at the

mouth with cheap soap, pretended to have been cast out of Bedlam with no place to go. A dummerer, a scroll tied about his neck to say he was deaf and dumb, stood making sounds so pitiful he deceived many passers-by, unless one should look inside the man's mouth, where his tongue was folded cunningly to produce the effect. Scattered among all of these were the doxies and dells, raucous as any of the men, each outdoing the others in her tale of hardship.

Near the end of the street was a sunburned, powerfully-built man who carried himself erect, though his clothes were as thin and patched as any of the others. This one commanded attention, for while he held a wooden bowl out before him, in which were a few small coins, he made no whining appeal, nor pretended to be sick. On the contrary, he looked Thomas in the eye like an equal, and as the three riders passed him, called out:

'A penny for an ex-soldier, sir, who has fought for his Queen against the papists!'

Thomas reined his mount, fumbling for his purse. Ahead of him, Catherine turned on her pony and cried in a frightened tone: 'Thomas, keep up or you'll lose your way!'

He found a groat and leaned down to place it in the man's bowl. The fellow nodded his thanks, with a knowing grin. He had a livid scar on the side of his neck.

'Been blooded yourself, master, if I'm not mistaken. Ireland, or the Low Countries?'

'Does it matter which?' Thomas answered, with a wry smile. The man rattled his bowl. 'Spare another penny, and I'll toast your health tonight.'

Thomas spread his hands. 'I'm but a servant.'

The man laughed. 'Then you're a well-mounted servant. Good luck to you.'

'And to you,' Thomas replied, and turned away. Peering ahead through the throng, and the smoke that drifted from the chimneys of the tightly-packed houses, he saw Catherine waving anxiously at him. In front, her mistress had halted and was looking back along the street. Thomas urged his horse forward until he drew level with them. Lady Margaret did not look pleased.

'I'm surprised you've money to throw away on beggars,' she said. 'Especially a ruffler, for that is what they call such as he. Is it not so?'

For some reason she looked angry - even bitter. He registered surprise that she should be aware of the street name of a class of beggar-folk. Rufflers - counterfeit ex-soldiers - considered themselves a cut above the rabble, and entitled to coin as of right. The highest caste of all beggars, the Upright Men, scorned to accept any other form of charity and strutted

47

the roads as if they were gentlemen, with their doxies at their heels like servants.

'He was a true ex-soldier, my lady,' Thomas said. 'I believe I know the look of them.'

'Then why doesn't he seek work?' Lady Margaret asked.

There was a moment's silence. Calmly, Thomas answered: 'Perhaps he has tried. There are many like him, with few places for them. And there'll be more about, now that we're at open war with the Spaniard.'

Lady Margaret looked keenly at him. Catherine sat staring from one to the other, amazed at the falconer's impertinence. No servant at Petbury would dare to answer her mistress back in such a manner. What was more startling, was that Lady Margaret seemed not to resent it, but merely said: 'We are almost at the house. Before us is Tower Street, with Sything Lane down on the left.'

Shaking the reins, she willed her high-spirited mare forward through the busy street, following a curve round towards St Dunstan's church whose bells were clanging, several minutes late. Tower Street opened on their right. At the far end the ditch rose, the great forbidding bulk of the Tower upon it with its onion domes high above them, the royal standard flying. Catherine almost cried out, overwhelmed by the sight. Off to their right, the river could be glimpsed down side-streets, flowing steadily here below the bridge, with barges and wherries moving upon it.

They turned finally into Sything Lane which was quieter, with large houses, walled about and gated. Some members of the Privy Council lived here, including the Secretary of State himself. Other properties belonged to Lords who spent much of the time at their country seats, coming rarely into town. Sir Robert was such a nobleman: when he inherited Petbury on the death of his father he had sold the town house.

The house of Francis Pickering, Lady Margaret's late father, stood halfway down the street, backing on to Tower Hill. It was of red brick, with a hawthorn tree at the front, and a tumbledown wall. The degree of neglect was shocking. The place had been empty for a long time; too long, Thomas thought, noting broken window panes and a chimney that leaned dangerously.

Lady Margaret sat on her horse in silence, gazing at the house of her childhood.

Thomas dismounted and started towards the gate, which was half-open. At that moment a man appeared, seemingly from nowhere, in a heavy woollen gown and a floppy, old-fashioned cap. Though he was elderly, with coarse grey hairs sprouting from his ears, his movements were as agile as those of a much younger man. He strode towards them, calling out: 'Lady Vicary?'

Lady Margaret motioned to Thomas, who came forward to help her dismount. Facing the man she said: 'You are Master Stocker.'

'Doctor Nicholas Stocker, my lady - a great honour,' the lawyer said, and doffed his cap to reveal a shining bald pate. 'I trust your journey has not been too tedious?'

Brushing the question aside, Lady Margaret asked: 'Why has no one cared for my brother's house?'

The lawyer quickly assumed a professional air. 'I regret that in such a matter, I am powerless. The house is no longer your brother's. I understood you were aware of that fact.'

'Am I now to know the name of the new owner?' Lady Margaret asked. Stocker shook his head gravely. 'I am unable to furnish that information, my lady. The sale was agreed through another party.'

Thomas, who had retained a respectful silence, thought he detected a crafty look behind the lawyer's pale, rheumy eyes. This man knew more than he cared to reveal.

'I had hoped,' Stocker said suddenly, 'that I would have the pleasure of dealing with your brother again. Please accept my condolences. A most unfortunate matter - a tragedy.'

Lady Margaret inclined her head, saying rather coolly: 'I am here in my brother's place, to settle his affairs.'

'There are loose ends,' Stocker agreed. 'But as your ladyship knows, you have no power of signature.'

There was a tense pause before Lady Margaret replied: 'I am the only surviving member of my family, Doctor Stocker.'

There was a bleakness in the lawyer's gaze, as he answered: 'You are quite certain of the fact, my lady?'

At that, she caught her breath. Thomas and Catherine watched a look come over her face that neither had seen before: one of plain fear.

Quickly, she recovered herself. 'I would like to see inside - shall we say for sentimental reasons. Is that possible?'

Stocker hesitated.

'Do you have a key?' Lady Margaret asked. The lawyer, with a smile of regret, said he did not - at which moment Thomas, who was beginning to take a powerful dislike to the man, said: 'There'd be no difficulty getting in, my lady. By the look of the place, one good thrust on the door would serve to force it open.'

Stocker's smile vanished. 'The house is private property,' he said. 'Breaking in would constitute a felony.'

'Doctor Stocker.' Lady Margaret's face softened into a winning smile. 'Surely you would not refuse the request of a bereaved woman to look over her childhood home, for the last time?'

There was a silence. Then Stocker said: 'Perhaps, if you gave your word you would merely look...'

'Of course,' Lady Margaret nodded.

'Then you will find the door unlocked,' Stocker said. 'In fact, the house has been ransacked.'

Placing his cap firmly on his head, he added: 'Permit me to call upon you, my lady. There are matters I should speak of - for your ears alone, naturally.' His gaze deliberately excluding Thomas, he waited.

'Come tomorrow afternoon, to Sir Marcus Brooke's house on the Strand,' Lady Margaret said coolly

Stocker inclined his head. 'Now if your ladyship will forgive me.' And turning on his heel, he walked rapidly away up the street, turned the corner and was gone.

Lady Margaret relaxed a little, though it was clear now she was somewhat shaken. Looking towards the house, she said: 'Shall we go inside?'

Thomas led the way to the heavy front door, which was badly scratched. Stocker had spoken truly: as he turned the iron handle the door opened on to a dim, damp-smelling hallway full of rubbish.

The house-tour was brief, and depressing. Catherine walked uneasily behind her mistress, as she picked her way over sticks of broken furniture, smashed crockery, rags of soiled linen, and curtains that were so mildewed they fell apart at the touch. Each room was a more distressing sight than the last: everything of value had vanished long since - even the newel post and balusters had been ripped out, rendering the stairs dangerous. Many windows were broken, and rain had come in for so long that the floorboards had started to rot in several places.

At the back of the house, Thomas found a surprisingly large room with tall windows and shelves that reached from floor to ceiling. There was no furniture, the shelves were warped in places and thick with dust - but it was the amount of broken glass that astonished him. It was everywhere. What had once been bottles and jars of blue, brown and clear glass, were smashed to pieces, almost covering the floor. There were stains of every hue on some of the fragments, and strange odours still clinging to them. In the fireplace, someone had burned a mass of papers; ash had spilled out on to the floor. As Thomas surveyed the sorry sight, standing in the middle of the room, Lady Margaret appeared in the doorway and said: 'This was my father's laboratory.'

She took a step into the room, adding: 'He was a man of science, Thomas. A brilliant alchemist, a geographer... he knew Martin Frobisher and John Hawkins - his mind stretched far beyond the shores of our little island, to the unknown reaches of the earth.'

Thomas watched her in silence.

'People feared him,' she continued, her voice rising, 'as they still do his old friend, the great Doctor Dee. They fear all men of deep learning and knowledge - they called him a sorcerer and a magus. Such stupidity.' Her tone was harsh. 'Had they known him as I did, they would have revered him not merely for his wisdom, but for his goodness and his humanity.'

Her gaze roved across the littered floor. 'Now the house is empty, they have vented their rage upon his workplace. It should not have been allowed to happen!'

There was a catch in her throat, but without shame she looked at Thomas and said: 'I hated my brother. Not for what he was - nor even for his failures... but because of—' she stopped herself.

Thomas, without thinking, had taken a step towards her, pity in his eyes. Too late, he realized how close he had drawn. He checked himself, cursing inwardly at his carelessness. He and Lady Margaret were less than a yard apart, their faces level. Surprised at his own temerity, Thomas looked into her eyes, which had filled with tears. To his further surprise, she returned his gaze, and leaned involuntarily towards him.

Then footsteps sounded from the hallway, and Catherine appeared, mumbling: 'I'm sorry my lady, I was only looking for the close stool, only if it's upstairs I fear to go there, it don't look safe to me...'

The poor girl faltered, a hand jerking of its own accord towards her mouth, at the spectacle of her mistress and Thomas the falconer, looking for all the world as if they were about to kiss.

But Lady Margaret turned gracefully to her maid and said: 'No matter, Catherine. We shall leave now.'

And pulling her cloak about her shoulders, she went from the glass-strewn room, Catherine following silently on her heels. As she went out, the maid looked at Thomas in sheer disbelief.

CHAPTER 5

When Lady Margaret and her two servants left the house and walked out to the street, a sharp-faced old woman in a frayed cap was standing by the next gateway. As they drew closer she asked excitedly: 'Are you the new owner, Madam?'

Lady Margaret shook her head and walked to her horse, but the old woman seemed to have no inhibition about engaging strangers in conversation. Looking hard at each of them she said: 'You've been inside - does it stink of the devil's farts, like they say?'

'It does not,' Thomas said to her. 'And my lady is tired. If you'll pardon us, we've had a long journey.'

Undeterred, the old woman gabbled: 'There was a wizard lived there - doing magic late at night, with potions in bottles. He kept a demon once - like an ape, it was!'

'Enough, mistress,' Thomas said with a frown, but Lady Margaret stopped dead, the colour draining from her face.

'It's the Lord's truth!' the old woman said, pointing a shaky finger towards the house. 'Twenty years or more back - I was housekeeper then, as I am now.'

Catherine, who had been looking on with disapproval, said: 'Where I come from housekeeper don't address a lady like that.'

The old woman scowled at her, but Lady Margaret fixed her with a gaze, and said: 'Do you not recognize me, Eliza Hall?'

The old woman started, then her eyes widened. 'Mistress Pickering! Is it you?'

Lady Margaret gave a thin smile. 'I'm the wizard's daughter. Now Lady Vicary.'

Considerably chastened, the old woman backed away saying: 'I had naught to do with it, my lady.'

'To do with what?' Lady Margaret asked. 'The wrecking of my father's laboratory?'

Frightened, the old woman mumbled: 'There's been all sorts coming and going here. Ever since last winter, when your brother...' She broke off and turned to go inside, saying: 'I meant no offence to you.'

Catherine tossed her head, but Lady Margaret said: 'Let me assure you, Eliza, there were never any demons in this house. Only men.'

Then she turned to her horse. Thomas came forward to help her into the saddle.

As they rode away down the street, Thomas glanced back to see the old woman peeping after them. Then seeing him, she darted back into the gateway like a squirrel.

Sir Marcus Brooke's fine house on the Strand, backing on to the river between Somerset

House and the Savoy, was secluded from the noisome city. Here the party were made mercifully welcome an hour later by a very different sort of housekeeper, a pleasant-faced younger woman with smiling eyes, who bobbed and announced herself as Jane Bull. Catherine, after another long ride back through London, was relieved to find a good room prepared for her and Lady Margaret, with clean beds and water for washing. She bustled about, none the worse for the day's excitement, seeing her mistress settled in and unpacking her clothes. Thomas, having stabled and fed the horses, sat in the big, warm kitchen while servants came and went. Lady Margaret would have a light supper and a glass of claret upstairs, Mistress Bull announced, sending the scullery-maids about their business when they giggled and looked sideways at the tall falconer. For Thomas there was hot broth and bread and a piece of beef, with pudding pie to follow, all of it washed down with good ale. He left not a shred on his trencher, then sat back at the long table and gave the housekeeper a grateful smile.

'I'm glad to find London ale as good as Berkshire brew,' he said.

The woman drew up a stool, saying she would be pleased to hear news of Sir Marcus and Lady Alice, who were due back from the country in a week or so. Every muscle in Thomas's body ached for sleep, but feeling it would be bad manners to excuse himself so soon, he settled down to talk. He soon found, however, that it was Jane Bull who liked to do the talking.

Sir Marcus it seemed, was seldom at home, always busy with some important matter or other. Lady Alice was a tyrant and a scold, and the servants dreaded her return. How she and Lady Margaret, who was such a sensitive soul, got on together, Jane couldn't imagine. Sir Robert and his wife had stayed as guests here, on rare visits to London. Sir Robert was thought a true gentleman, though he had his ways.

Thomas was attentive now. On the journey back, he had tried not to think of that moment alone with his mistress in the glass-strewn laboratory. But not for a minute had the vision of her face left him: her face close to his - not forbidding, but challenging, even daring him.

Lady Margaret of course, Jane Bull continued cheerfully, was a lucky woman, being the daughter of a penniless gentleman. A scholar of some sort, old Francis was, widowed when his children were still young, and spending all his time with his books and experiments. But Thomas must have heard all the talk? Seemed the young Margaret had no dowry to bring, yet she was never short of suitors being such a beautiful woman - though none so rich as Sir Robert Vicary. Sir Robert was bowled over as soon as he saw her, folk said, and though he

was twelve years her senior - she would be around twenty years of age when they married, wasn't that so? - she was glad to have him, and who wouldn't be? Though, looking back, and it must be eighteen years now, she'd never looked happy, they said, not on her wedding day nor since, even when the children came, and both of them healthy and good-looking as she. Seemed some folk just didn't know when they were well-off.

'The marriage was arranged,' Thomas told her.

Jane Bull smiled at him. 'They always are between nobles and gentry, aren't they? You name me one that wasn't.'

He nodded absently. He had served as Lady Margaret's falconer since the day she came as a young bride to Petbury, yet at times he felt he knew little about her. He looked up to see Jane Bull rising from the table to take down another mug from the board. She wouldn't normally think to indulge, she said, sitting down again, but mistress was away and neither of them were getting any younger, were they? She smiled as he filled her mug and raised his own to drink her health. Her eyes fixed on his over the rim.

'She's a deep one, isn't she?' Jane remarked. 'Lady Margaret? But not a mean woman. You wouldn't think she and that brother of hers were of the same blood.'

He was surprised that she should know anything of Nathaniel Pickering; perhaps news travelled more easily in London. Jane had never seen the man, she admitted: he had not been a guest here. Sir Marcus would have naught to do with him and Sir Robert only tolerated him because he was family. He was a sot, she said, taking a generous pull from her mug, and a wastrel and Lord-knew-what-else. It was no surprise he came to a bad end. She leaned closer to Thomas across the well-scrubbed board. 'They say he went with boys, as well as maids.'

Thomas smiled faintly, wanting to turn the conversation again to Lady Margaret. Jane leaned back slightly, without taking her eyes off his. There were other rumours, going back to when Lady Margaret was married and before, she said, adding: 'They say she was giving her brother money. Because he knew things that could hurt her, if he told Sir Robert.'

'What sort of things?' he asked, stifling a yawn and glancing involuntarily about the kitchen. It looked now as if all the other servants, whether by chance or design, had gone to bed. Outside night had fallen, and here he and Jane Bull sat alone at the big table, talking low by firelight.

'That's enough talk of them, isn't it?' Jane said. 'What's past is past. Here we are in the present, you and me.'

He was wide awake now, and cold sober, as the housekeeper laid a hand on his and said

softly: 'I'm a widow, falconer. Past my forty years, but I enjoy a bit of company. What of you?'

'I'm a widower,' he admitted, and suddenly Mary Finbow's face rose up in his mind, and his breath caught in his throat.

'In the Lord's name,' he murmured, 'what am I doing?'

Jane, taken aback for a moment, paused, then said: 'I've my own room above, top of the back stairs. It's tiny but it's quiet.'

He had been so keen to talk of Lady Margaret that he had barely realized what was happening. He struggled to make sense of his muddled thoughts. Lady Margaret, his dead wife - the two of them, he suddenly realized, were equally beyond his reach.

Jane Bull watched him with a sly look. She was a knowing one, he thought, and said to her: 'Mayhap this is hard to believe, but I've not been with anyone else since my wife died.'

'How long's that?' she asked.

'Three years, almost.'

She kept her hand on his, saying; 'I've been a widow since eighty-two. It was a plague year.' She looked away for a moment. 'My husband was Sir Marcus's farrier; a jealous man. But nothing I do can hurt him now, can it?'

Thomas took her hand and held it. 'A little company might not be such a bad thing at that,' he said, and rose to his feet. She got to hers too, facing him across the table. They passed along its length, holding hands across it; then reaching the end, arms about each other, they walked towards the stairs.

In the early hours of the morning, Thomas awoke with a feeling of unease. There was very little light in the room; for a moment he thought he was back at Petbury in his own bed. Then he heard a scream, and another, and realized what it was that had woken him. Throwing the coverlet aside, he stumbled to his feet and groped for the door. The screams came not through the small window: they were here in the house.

It was so dark in the passage that he crashed into something - a chest of some sort. Gritting his teeth, he moved along to where the passage turned and gave on to the main landing. Dim light showed under a door at the far end - from which now came the raised voices of women, one of them hysterical. He ran forward and fumbled for the handle, to find the door locked from within. There was another scream when he rattled it, so he called out quickly: 'My lady -

it's Thomas! Are you hurt?'

There was a moment, then lowered voices; then the door was unlocked and thrown wide,

and Catherine stood there in her shift, holding a candle in a shaking hand.

'There was someone at the window! They tried to break in!'

Without a thought he pushed past her, to see Lady Margaret standing beside a great curtained four-poster bed, pulling a gown over her nightclothes.

'My lady - ' he began, then froze and blushed to the roots of his hair. He did not look down, but stared straight ahead, as if afraid to confirm what he now remembered: that he was wearing only a shirt that reached barely to his thighs.

But at once the silence was broken by doors banging from the direction of the servants' quarters, followed by anxious voices. Jane Bull appeared at the doorway, saying quickly: 'I'll attend to her ladyship, master falconer. You'd best dress yourself - and make a search of the house,' she added, as Thomas, with a swift look of gratitude, muttered his acquiescence and disappeared through the door.

He hurried along the landing, as Sir Marcus Brooke's servants gathered, among them a young groom with a candlestick in his hand. 'What's the coil?' he asked, rubbing sleep from his eyes.

'Someone tried to break into her ladyship's room,' Thomas replied. 'Let me get my clothes on, and we'll meet downstairs.'

'Hadn't we best call the constable?' the groom said, not seeming to relish the prospect of confronting a gang of burglars.

'Send word if you like,' Thomas said. 'I'm going to look round the garden. Can you get a lantern?'

The young man turned to go and Thomas fumbled his way back to Jane Bull's room, relieved to be able to close the door behind him. He dressed quickly, then made his way down to the kitchen, where candles burned and someone had poked the glowing embers of the fire into life. The groom, who was lighting a lantern from a taper, looked up at him with a puzzled frown, saying; 'No one can gain entry into this house. The gates and walls are high, and spiked as well. Sure her ladyship wasn't having a bad dream? You know what women are.'

'She's not easily frightened,' Thomas told him. 'They both saw something, I believe - she and the maid.'

There was a pistol on the table. The groom picked it up and fumbled with it, saying: 'It's the master's. Not loaded, but it might scare 'em.'

The two of them went out through the yard door and began a search of the grounds. They

saw and heard nothing, except the lapping of the Thames close by - like other noblemen's houses west of the city, that of Sir Marcus had private stairs leading down to the water. From across the river, on Bankside, came distant sounds of revelry, even in the middle of the night.

On the far side of the house, they stood beneath the windows of the bedroom occupied by Lady Margaret and her maid. Working the lantern, Thomas peered about the flower-beds - and almost at once found boot-prints in the earth. Raising the lantern high, he saw that thick ivy covered the entire wall to the edges of the casements, providing an easy enough foothold for a determined climber. Fronds of it hung loose, as if torn from the wall.

'It don't make any sense,' the groom was saying. 'An upstairs window's not the place for seeking an entry. Leastways,' he added, 'It's not the way I'd work, if I were planning to rob a house like this.'

He grinned, uneasy about how his words sounded. But Thomas said: 'Nor me. I'd be forcing a kitchen door, looking for the knives and the best plate.'

'That's the way of it,' the groom said. 'And in any case, how did they get over the wall?'

They walked across the lawns, past rose-beds and arched bowers. The high garden walls would have been difficult to scale without a ladder. There were no signs of damage anywhere, nor any other footprints.

'That leaves the stairs,' Thomas said. The two men walked to the end of the garden, through the small water-gate and out on to the top step. Below them the river gleamed thick and black in the lantern-light. There was no sign of a boat.

'High tide,' the groom remarked. 'If there was someone, he could have got away quick enough.' He stifled a yawn. 'What now, master falconer?'

Thomas shrugged. 'If I were you I'd go back to bed. I'll go and see what her ladyship wants me to do.'

In the house, things had calmed down somewhat. Jane Bull had taken a drink of hot punch up to Lady Margaret, and was in the kitchen having a small one herself when Thomas and the groom came in. Her ladyship had retired, but Catherine would sit up the rest of the night.

Lady Margaret had asked that someone remain outside the door of their room, ready to come at once if either of them should call.'

Thomas sighed and nodded, suddenly aware of his weariness. The groom mumbled a goodnight and went off to his bed. Jane got up from the table and went quickly to Thomas, saying: 'She knows naught of our being together.' She raised her face up to his. He kissed her gently, then moved towards the stairs.

The next morning, there was much excitement in the house after the events of the night. Thomas, sitting in a chair on the landing outside Lady Margaret's room, fell asleep towards dawn, and was woken abruptly an hour or so later by Catherine unbolting the door close to his ear. There had been no further incident, he was told. Getting stiffly to his feet, he followed the maid down to the kitchen, where Jane Bull was firmly in command. Breakfast was ready for Lady Margaret, but Catherine said her ladyship wanted nothing but a cup of warm milk. Turning to Thomas, who was seating himself at the table, she said: 'My lady has errands for us both today. You're to go with her into London to buy the falcon.'

Her mistress, Catherine said to the room in general, would not be diverted from finishing her business, no matter what had happened. She gave Thomas a hard stare and added: 'We're her trusted servants and should never forget it. For my part I'd spare no pains on her behalf.'

She walked across the kitchen to get the milk. There was a new spring to her step, Thomas thought, and wondered at the cause of it.

CHAPTER 6

Directly after breakfast the constable called at the house, a fat man of limited imagination to match his limited powers. There was little he could do except offer to keep an eye on the place. He had asked the bellman who was abroad during the night, but the man had seen and heard nothing untoward. Though robberies were common enough, the constable had never known anyone try to gain entry to Sir Marcus's house. Sir Marcus should be informed. No doubt her ladyship would be returning to the country, after her fright?

Lady Margaret replied that she had no such intention, and after dismissing the constable, ordered Thomas to hail a waterman for the journey downriver. The morning was fine and sunny; today at least they would be able to travel in some comfort.

On the Thames, with the loud-voiced watermen plying their trade, ferrying people up and down the river or across to the Southwark shore, Thomas was somewhat ill-at-ease in Lady Margaret's company. She had said little about the events of last night, only that she and Catherine had been awakened by a noise at the window and had seen someone outside. It was too dark to make out any detail, but whoever it was rapped on the pane, causing Catherine to break into hysterics - the screams had been hers.

'If you'll allow, my lady,' Thomas said, as they scudded along with the roar of the city to their left, 'I don't believe whoever it was meant to get into your room at all.'

'How should that be?' Lady Margaret asked.

'They would be too easily discovered. It shows a recklessness that doesn't sit well with the way they got into the garden, and out again.'

'Perhaps,' Lady Margaret said, gazing past him over the sparkling surface of the water, 'it was merely an attempt to frighten me.'

He had thought as much himself. But how would the intruder have known which room Lady Margaret was in - or even where she was staying? Why, in any case, would someone want to frighten her?

'No matter,' Lady Margaret said then. 'It's over with, and no harm was done.'

'Thanks be to God, my lady,' Thomas said. He thought to add that perhaps she should change rooms, but at that moment the waterman, a rough, leather-skinned fellow with a bushy beard, paused at his oars and addressed Lady Margaret.

'You'll want to alight this side of the bridge, my lady. Then walk round to the Keys by Thames Street.'

Lady Margaret regarded the man with a hint of a smile. 'Must we? Are you afraid to shoot
the waters?'

The man frowned slightly. 'Afraid? I've been taking my boat under that bridge in all weathers, for more 'n twenty years.'

'Then we are in safe hands,' she answered. 'I've engaged you for as far as the Legal Keys, and that is where we will go.'

'As you please,' the waterman said, and leaned on his oars.

Ahead of them the massive bulk of old London Bridge loomed, with the great three-storey houses of merchants and tradesmen built upon it, rooftops gleaming in the morning sun. The current was racing now, the waters soon to be cleaved by the 'starlings', the tapered stone islands that supported the nineteen great piers of the bridge. They acted almost as a dam on the Thames, which rushed between the piers like a cataract into the Pool, the calmer reaches below. Only the hardiest souls shot the waters under the arches, and only in good conditions. Lady Margaret, with the breeze blowing at her hood, had a light in her eye that Thomas recognized: the same look she wore when they rode fast on the Downs on a clear morning, chasing the soaring falcons.

Now the bridge rushed towards them, the din of the foot-traffic upon it drowned by the roar of the waters. The waterman shipped his oars and steadied himself, shouting: 'Hold on tight now!' - and they were borne between the starlings on the rushing current, under the vast echoing arch, dropping several feet like a log being washed down some chalkhill beck. Then they emerged into sunshine and calmer water, and the bridge was behind them.

All three of them were wet, and Lady Margaret was laughing - the first time Thomas had seen her in such a humour, he realized, for many weeks. The spray was on her cheeks as she turned to him in sheer exhilaration. Then their eyes met, and he dropped his gaze.

The waterman had brought his wherry quickly about to larboard and was sculling towards the Legal Keys where everything from wool to fish was shipped in and out. Here, the great cargo-ships and galleons rode at anchor; lighters took goods ashore. Before them, the myriad noises of the wharves filled the air. Drawing close to the nearest set of rickety, water-worn stairs, the man held his craft fast to allow his passengers to alight. Thomas stepped out first and extended a hand to help Lady Margaret ashore. As she climbed on to the step, she held out a shilling to the waterman.

'That's for your pains - and my pleasure.' The man took the coin, grinned broadly and doffed his hat. 'I'll drink your health tonight, my lady,' he called, and pushed expertly off into the stream

Threading their way along the crowded waterfront, with the smell of fish and tar and a hundred other scents assailing them, Lady Margaret and Thomas walked the short distance to Botolph Key where the dealer in birds had his shop. Thomas had been relieved when his mistress announced that they would go together; he no longer wished to let her out of his sight.

The shop was kept by a broad-faced Dutchman, who bowed gravely to Lady Margaret and gave his name as Henry van Velsen. Stolidly he ushered her through a forest of wicker cages filled with shrilling and squawking birds of many kinds, from larks for the table to choughs and ravens for pets. There was even a green parrot, brought in by sailors from some far-off land. Droppings carpeted the floor; the stench was overpowering.

At the rear was a row of larger cages, inside which were four of the most magnificent falcons Thomas had ever seen.

The gyrfalcons, larger than any of the birds at Petbury, were slightly darker than English falcons, but the speckled down on their chests was fine as ermine. Each had a thick hook on its top bill, and black eyes that peered intently through the bars.

Lady Margaret turned to the dealer. 'My falconer, Master Finbow, will take a closer look.'

The Dutchman nodded and gestured towards the cages. 'They is komm from Norvege, from the mountains. Passage birds, moulted once - fine hunters, all. You must reclaim them for the chase.'

Thomas looked keenly at each bird in turn. They were indeed haggards - wild falcons, that would need a lot of training. Two were females, the other, smaller ones, males or tercels. Both females were alert, blinking in the dim light. One of them had a slight caste in the eye, and an edgy look about her. The other sat motionless on her perch, staring back at him with a defiant air. He was about to suggest this one for purchase, when Lady Margaret spoke suddenly.

'I dislike seeing creatures of any sort caged. Especially in a place like this.' She addressed the dealer shortly. 'How long have they been here?'

The man looked displeased. 'All my birds well-fed, well cared-for,' he said. 'In Nederlands I deal in hawks, before Spanish come. Van Velsen famous for his hawks.'

'We'll have them all,' Lady Margaret said.

The man raised an eyebrow. 'Is twelve shillings for each bird.'

'Very well,' she answered briskly, and glanced at Thomas, who had remained silent. 'Will you take them as they are?'

After a moment, he nodded. 'If I can get them safely back to Berkshire, my lady.'

She turned to van Velsen. 'If I pay you a further sixpence for each hawk, will you keep them here until I send for them?'

The dealer nodded his head, with a trace of a smile; this lady was not one to argue with.

'Then our business is concluded.' Drawing her purse from her cloak, Lady Margaret counted out sovereigns, florins and sixpences to the value of two pounds and ten shillings, and handed them to the Dutchman, who bowed his thanks.

'Now we will go,' she said. 'The air here is fetid.'

And after giving the man her name, she swept outside with Thomas at her heels. She did not speak again until they were in another boat, being rowed upriver towards Sir Marcus's house.

It was midday by the time they returned. Lady Margaret gave word that she would receive Master Nicholas Stocker that afternoon, and took her dinner alone. Catherine and Thomas had theirs at the long kitchen table with the other servants. There was momentous news from the city: Mary Stuart, the Queen of Scots, was to be tried for treason and conspiracy to murder the Queen. The Lord High Admiral, Lord Howard of Effingham, was commissioner of the trial. Though it was long expected, since the execution last month of the papist Anthony Babington and his fellow plotters, there was great excitement round the table. Sir Marcus, it seemed, was an acquaintance of Lord Howard, one of the richest men in England. He had a house upriver at Chelsea, and was sometimes seen on the water in the royal barge, accompanying the Queen on her progresses.

Thomas said little during the meal. His concerns were more immediate: how to deal with four wild gyrfalcons. His mistress could, on occasions, be impulsive. As he finished his dinner and was about to leave, the gossip turned to lighter matters. Jane Bull said to him:

'There was a beggar came to the gate this morning, acting the fool. Laughing all the time like he was sun-touched.'

'Naught wrong with him,' said James, the young groom, wiping his trencher clean with a hunk of bread. 'He was an Abraham man. That's how they get their living, instead of working like the rest of us.'

'You should 'a seen what he was wearing,' one of the kitchen maids said to Catherine. 'A saffron coat!'

Thomas froze, halfway out of his seat. 'A coat of yellow?'

The girl nodded. 'Stood out like a buttercup in a midden. Mayhap he likes to get himself noticed.'

'Likely stole it off some gentleman,' James said, with a look at Thomas. The falconer was

staring into thin air. Into his mind came a picture of the coroner's inquest at Petbury, and an old man giving testimony that on the day Nathaniel Pickering was killed, he had seen a vagrom man in a yellow coat.

'You ever seen anyone in a coat like that before?' he asked Jane.

She shook her head. 'Why d'you ask that?'

'Curious, nothing more.' As he left the table, he noticed Catherine and James exchanging secret glances. Seeing his gaze, Catherine gave him a pouting look and tossed her head.

That afternoon Thomas was sent for by Lady Margaret, to a hall overlooking the garden where she sat ready to receive Nicholas Stocker. To his surprise, she asked him to remain with her during the meeting.

'I want a witness present,' she told him. Then she added: 'You recall that when we left Petbury my husband bade you trust Doctor Stocker. But then, he had never set eyes on him. The man was known only to my late brother.'

She was seated by a small table. Shafts of sunlight caught the dust and lanced across the room on to the smooth stone floor at her feet.

'You do not trust this man, Thomas - any more than I do.'

He remained silent, but half to herself, she said: 'There are matters to be cleared up. More perhaps, than I expected.'

Then she looked at him, and he lowered his eyes. Ever since the moment when they had been alone together in her father's house, he had found himself unable to return her gaze.

'Dear Thomas,' she said softly.

'Whatever your fears, my lady, I swear I'd -' He began, then shut his mouth at once. But she smiled.

'I know that.'

At that moment the elderly serving-man arrived to announce Nicholas

Stocker. Lady Margaret nodded for him to be shown in.

Today the lawyer wore a gown richly-trimmed with fur, deep blue hose and new shoes with wide buckles. He came in, bowed his greetings, then half-turned towards Thomas, with a questioning look at Lady Margaret. When she explained the reason for his presence the man was more than merely surprised, he was uneasy, though he tried to conceal it under a thin smile.

'These are not matters to be spoken of before servants, my lady.'

'Thomas has served me faithfully all my married life,' Lady Margaret replied. 'He has my

trust, and that of my husband. We value his counsel second only to that of our steward.'

But Stocker was not about to give in. Lowering his voice, he said: 'Your ladyship may regret having allowed me to air these things before him.'

She paused. 'What can you be speaking of?'

He waited, then seeing she would not change her mind, said rather harshly: 'I speak of your brother's debts.'

'They are no secret,' Lady Margaret answered.

'Very well; then I will proceed.' He took a sealed document from his wide sleeve and held it out. 'I must tell you that the debts have been bought up by a third party.'

She was taken aback. 'Which party is that?'

'I cannot say.'

'You choose not to.'

'I cannot choose.' The lawyer's smile had all but disappeared now. He was a cold adversary, Thomas thought, and not to be underestimated.

Lady Margaret considered. 'This party - is it the same one which

71

bought the house in Sything Lane?'

Stocker gave the slightest of shrugs.

'Doctor Stocker,' Lady Margaret said, 'my husband is fully prepared to settle any of my brother's outstanding debts. But how is that to be, if we do not know to whom they shall be paid?'

'You may pay me the total sum, as set down here,' Stocker said. 'I will then ensure that all debts are settled.'

Thomas, standing near the window, gave a barely audible snort, but Lady Margaret, shaking her head slightly, said to Stocker: 'How can I be certain you will carry out the business?' Stocker bristled. 'I am a Doctor of Laws, a graduate of the Middle Temple, Lady Vicary. I have a reputation.' He tossed the document on to the table.

Instead of growing heated, Lady Margaret ignored the paper and put on one of her most

disarming smiles. 'I don't doubt it. Nevertheless, you will understand that I find your revelations surprising, not to say strange.'

But Stocker was immune to the charms of any woman. He stared back blandly and said: 'It is my duty to advise you, my lady, that you would be wise not to enquire too deeply into this matter.'

Lady Margaret's smile faded. 'Do you threaten me, sir?'

'Of course not,' Stocker answered quickly, then added: 'I speak merely of things best left untouched - indeed, best forgotten. Your ladyship knows, perhaps, which way my mind moves.'

For the first time, Lady Margaret lowered her gaze. Thomas thought of the moment outside her father's house the day before, when Stocker had seemingly frightened her with a hint of some kind. What it might refer to, he could not begin to guess.

'I understand you enjoyed my late brother's confidence, Doctor

Stocker,' Lady Margaret said, raising her eyes to meet his.

'I had that honour, my lady,' the lawyer replied.

'Tell me, did you always find him a truthful man?'

The question irked him. 'I had no reason to doubt his word.'

'And no reason, I am sure, for him to doubt yours.'

'I find the implication of that remark difficult to bear, my lady,' Stocker said stiffly. But Lady Margaret smiled again. The duel was not yet lost, and Thomas, watching with concealed admiration, willed her to press her advantage.

'Your employment as my brother's lawyer ceased some time before his death, I would guess.'

Stocker looked slightly contemptuous. 'He had no funds left with which to pay me. And I am but one of his creditors.'

'And naturally, you require settlement of your account.'

'Naturally enough,' Stocker replied drily.

'Was my brother's house mortgaged, Doctor Stocker?'

On this question, Stocker allowed his silence to be taken as confirmation.

'Well.' Lady Margaret took a breath. 'You seem determined to leave me mewed up, with just the one exit.'

'Forgive me, Lady Vicary,' Stocker replied, 'but what does it matter by whose hand the debts are paid, so long as the slate is wiped clean?'

Lady Margaret's eyes flashed suddenly. 'You think the slate is wiped clean so easily as that?'

Stocker seemed to feel he had scored a minor hit. His tight smile returning, he merely said: 'I cannot imagine what it is your ladyship refers to.'

Thomas saw then her distress, underneath the guise of haughtiness. He tried to think of

some way to intervene. But Lady Margaret was not finished Without taking her eyes off Stocker, she picked the document up from the table and held it out to him. 'I must have time to consider.'

He frowned. 'What is there to consider, my lady? The debts must be paid, or a suit may be issued against your brother's next of kin. Since he left no heirs and you have no legal power in this matter, it may be sworn against your husband. I doubt Sir Robert would wish to find himself taken under guard to the Counter.'

Thomas froze. The thought of a wealthy knight like Sir Robert Vicary being marched to the debtor's prison like a commoner, was preposterous. He marvelled at Stocker's nerve. So, it seemed, did Lady Margaret. But keeping her voice low, she answered: 'I think that would be unlikely. Sir Robert is not without influence.'

'In that matter, Lady Vicary,' the lawyer replied, 'he may find at the final turn, that he has less than he thought.' Stepping forwards, he swept the document from her hand and thrust it into his sleeve.

'I have clients to attend upon at Westminster Hall,' he said brusquely. 'With your ladyship's permission I will return in two days' time. I trust then you will find it in your heart to give me satisfaction.'

'I cannot call to mind my plans for that day,' Lady Margaret said. 'But do rest assured sir, I shall send word to you as soon as I may. Now will you permit Thomas to show you out?'

She glanced at Thomas, who stepped forward. Ignoring him, Stocker turned and strode out of the room.

That night, Thomas declined Jane Bull's whispered invitation to come to her room after everyone was abed. Lady Margaret expected him to be in the male servants' quarters; if he should be sent for, for whatever reason. The housekeeper nodded and bade him goodnight, taking her end of candle on a dish towards the back stairs. Before disappearing, she threw him a look which, told him plainly she believed not one word of what he had said.

With a feeling of foreboding Thomas went to bed, but lay awake long after the other men commenced snoring on either side of him. When he finally fell asleep it was near dawn, and sounds of daybreak were rising from every direction.

It seemed only minutes later that Thomas heard anxious voices and found himself being shaken roughly awake, to be told that Lady Margaret wanted to see him at once. A message had arrived from the Dutchman, to say that a dreadful crime had been committed: the four gyrfalcons had been savagely killed.

CHAPTER 7

He found her standing by the window in the chamber where she had received Stocker the day before. As he came in, still dazed by the news, she said: 'Thomas, I have never believed in coincidence. This brutality was directed at me.'

He stared at her. 'Did the message say how it happened?'

She shook her head 'Someone broke into his shop during the night. They touched nothing else. Do you see?'

'But my lady...' He was at a loss for words. 'What meaning could it have? What purpose?'

'To frighten me. Like the intruder at the window. To drive me away, back to Petbury, perhaps.'

'By killing the hawks?' He shook his head. He found it difficult to understand how anyone could do this thing.

'Will you go there?' she said. 'Take one of the men with you if you like.'

'Of course, my lady.' He hesitated. 'Do you have any other instructions for me?'

She was staring out of the window, across the garden. 'I suppose the prudent course would be for us to return to Petbury and place the matter in my husband's hands. He'll settle Nathaniel's debts, pat me on the head and tell me not to concern myself. We can go hawking on the Downs, and forget any unpleasantness we have encountered here.'

He waited, until she turned towards him with a weak smile. 'Would that be your advice, master falconer?'

He smiled. 'I'm honoured you should ask it, my lady.'

'Then speak,' Lady Margaret said.

He stared at the floor. It was surely too great a coincidence that the crime should have occurred directly after Lady Margaret had bought the birds. But how... An eerie notion struck him. He tried to dismiss it as foolishness, whereupon Lady Margaret spoke impatiently.

'Tell me your thoughts.'

'That we have been watched, every step of the way, since we reached London.'

She merely nodded and turned away. After a moment, she said quietly: 'Thomas, you were my husband's man before I came to Petbury. I have no right to ask of you what I will ask nevertheless.'

'Whatever you ask of me, my lady, you know I will do it.'

'Help me.'

He met her gaze. 'Tell me how.'

She had grown uneasy, as if weighing some sort of risk. But she seemed to have resolved to confide in him. He saw it then: there was nobody else she could trust.

'There may be someone who... wants to do me harm. For reasons I cannot - matters I had thought were over and forgotten. Until my brother...' She trailed off. 'The terrible fact is, I know not who they are. Or where they lie.'

'My lady, do you mean that your life may be in danger?'

She gave a slight shrug. 'They killed Nathaniel.'

He frowned. 'Who did?'

She said nothing, but he pressed her. 'Then, will you tell me why?' He had forgotten his reserve, so intent was he on learning the truth.

With a sudden harshness, she said: 'The curious part of it is - do you know who had most to gain from my brother's death?'

He shook his head.

'I did.' She began pacing the room, working her hands in a manner that was utterly unlike her.

'He threatened to tell my husband of things known only to the two of us. Matters I thought had been done with twenty years ago, before my marriage. I had to buy his silence - pay for his dicing and his bowling and his nights at the trugging-house... Whoever shot him off his horse saved me, and my secret. Until now.'

She stopped by the fireplace and leaned her head against the cool stone. 'I did a terrible thing, Thomas. Long ago.'

Never had he seen her so unnerved. He sought to find words of comfort. 'We make many mistakes when we are young, my lady.'

'I was young, yes,' Lady Margaret said, with her back to him. 'And wilful, and...' She was close to tears. 'Now I'm at a loss to know what I should do.'

'The lawyer,' he murmured. 'He knows more than he chose to tell you.'

She turned from the fireplace with a bitter look. 'No doubt be does, but he is not the enemy. He merely wants his money.'

'My lady.' Emboldened, he took a step towards her. 'Let me delve into this, discover what I can.' He paused. 'If you wish me to.'

He watched her gathering her thoughts. With a frown, she said: 'There will be danger. And we have only a few days before Sir Marcus and Lady Brooke return to London. With them here, it would be impossible.'

She looked at him then, with the light of challenge in her eyes. 'Are you willing to help me get to the nub of it? Whether it be a conspiracy, or merely vengeance they want?'

He nodded.

'And if we discover all, will you swear to keep my secret?'

Seeing the question that was forming, she forestalled him. 'I have broken no laws, I swear to you. I have harmed no one, but myself... and my late father.' She lowered her eyes suddenly. 'I broke his dear, gentle heart.'

She did weep, then, suddenly and uncontrollably, standing before him. And before he could stop himself, Thomas had crossed the few feet that separated them and folded her in his arms.

She did not prevent him, but cried against his shoulder. When the sobs subsided, she raised her head and met his gaze.

Things had gone too far now, but he no longer cared. To his joy neither, it seemed, did she. He bent and kissed her on the mouth, and she returned the kiss. Then she said: 'I hope you do not consider this your payment.'

'If so, it's payment enough.'

She drew back, suddenly brisk. She was herself again. 'Go now, to the dealer. Find out what you can. I will tell the household that we must stay longer to look for another falcon. In the meantime there are, perhaps, things I may do.'

As he turned to go, she said: 'I know you will not betray me.'

He smiled and walked from the room.

By mid-morning, Thomas, accompanied by James the groom, had taken a wherry downriver and made his way to Botolph Key off Thames Street, to the premises of Henry van Velsen.

When they walked inside, the Dutchman was sitting on a wooden box at the far end of the shop, surrounded by the shrilling of birds. He looked up with an expression of helplessness.

'I pay your mistress back,' he said. 'Hawks were in my care, I know that.'

Looking down at him, Thomas could not find it in himself to be brusque with the man. He was clearly numbed by the event.

'Tell me all that happened. Her ladyship wishes to know.'

The Dutchman spread his hands. 'What is to tell? I come down at daybreak, the door is forced open. I come in, the falcons are dead. Necks broken.'

Thomas glanced over the man's shoulder. 'May we look?'

The Dutchman shrugged, but made no move to prevent them. Thomas stepped past him to

the open doors of the cages and looked inside, his gorge rising at the sickening sight.

The gyrfalcons lay on the floor, their proud necks twisted and snapped. There were clear indications that they had resisted: feathers littered the cages, and blood was spattered in several places - human blood, Thomas guessed: the falcons had no doubt slashed and hacked at their attacker. Blood stained the beak of one of them, and the talons of two others.

'Whoever the whoreson bastards were, I hope they got their eyes clawed out.' James stood behind him, shocked at the savagery of the deed.

Thomas shook his head. 'They'd have worn masks, if they'd any sense. Gauntlets too. They knew what to do. Even so, the birds took their toll - see the blood.'

'I've seen enough,' James said, turning away. 'I'll wait for you outside.' With head bowed, the young groom shouldered his way through the swinging cages and out of the shop.

Thomas took a closer look. As he scanned the bars, perches and floors of the cages, a tiny glint caught his eye. He stooped to inspect one of the dead falcons, and saw a small gold ring on its talon. He took the ring off and examined it closely. It was a man's earring, torn from his flesh by the bird in its struggle. Whoever owned it, had paid for his deed with no little pain, perhaps. With a last look around, Thomas placed the ring inside his coat and moved back towards the Dutchman. The man had risen to his feet and was casting about, as if in search of something to do.

'Have you told the constables?' Thomas asked.

Van Velsen gave him a bleak look. 'What they can do? Hawks are dead.'

'There must have been a noise. Those birds fought like the devil. Did nobody hear anything?'

The man only shrugged.

'Have you asked your neighbours?' Thomas persisted, but the Dutchman was tired of his questions. He wore a hard expression.

'I am Dutch,' he said. 'Neighbours don't like me.' He indicated a man who had appeared at the entrance. 'Now I got customers. I nothing more to tell.'

Thomas followed him to the front of the shop. Van Velsen turned then, and said: 'I burn hawks now. Tell ladyship, I pay back her money.'

'It's not the money that concerns her,' Thomas answered. 'As for me, I want to find whoever did this.'

The Dutchman suddenly put out a large hand and gripped his arm.

'You find 'em, bring here, tell me,' he said. 'I choke them good, like they choke my hawks!'

Then he dropped his hand and turned away. Thomas walked out into the narrow street, where James stood waiting.

He did not go back to Sir Marcus's house, but told James he would make some enquiries, alone. The groom did not care to argue, but said he would return at once to Lady Margaret and tell her what they had found. He and Thomas parted at the end of Botolph's Key by the waterfront. As James walked off towards Bridge Street, Thomas turned back towards van Velsen's shop.

He was thoughtful. Now that he had observed the scene of cruelty, he was beginning to get some sense of the kind of people he might be up against. The notion that they could be connected with Lady Margaret in any way at all, bothered him considerably. What had a lady of her class and sensibility to do with such evildoers? For he believed, now, that the slaughter of the falcons was aimed deliberately at Lady Margaret. Why was no other bird harmed, and none stolen? It was an act of vile cruelty, akin to one of vengeance.

She had mentioned vengeance - but whose? She had confided in him so much, and yet told him so little. He knew that his heart was ruling his head in the entire matter. In his mind's eye he still saw her face, and tasted the warmth of her kiss.

With a deep breath, he plunged into the busy thoroughfare and began asking at the shops of the traders nearby. They were all busy men, and they had little to tell him. Word had got around of the attack on the Dutchman's falcons of course - it was a bad business, but nobody knew anything more of the matter. To his innocent question about suspicious-looking characters in the street, there was a roar of laughter from van Velsen's neighbour, a wool dealer, in which his apprentices, customers and even passers-by soon joined. If Thomas wanted to find suspicious characters, he was told, he had only to walk a few yards in any direction, and there they would be in abundance.

'This is London, master,' the dealer said, wiping his eyes with a greasy hand. 'Best get yourself back to the country, before someone cuts your purse-strings - and your breeches too.'

With a weak smile Thomas turned away and threaded his way to the top end of Botolph Key, where it opened on to Thames Street. People walked by in all directions: servants buying fish for their masters' tables, dealers and merchants doing business. With a feeling of helplessness, he looked about for a cheap ordinary where he might take his dinner and collect his thoughts. He asked a passer-by, and was directed to cross Thames Street, walk up Botolph Lane, then cut through an alley on the left into Pudding Lane, where he would find several eating-houses.

As Thomas turned into the narrow alley, which was choked with rotting and smelly refuse, there came a sound from behind. He whirled around, just in time to see a heavily-built man in a Spanish leather jerkin bearing down upon him, with an oak billet raised high above his head.

There was no time even to shout. He dodged aside, then hissed with pain as the club missed his head and crashed down upon his shoulder. Then he was grappling with his assailant, who cursed and blasphemed like the devil himself.

Thomas was the stronger, he began to realize, for the man was flabby, and soon sweat was running down his face. Hooking a leg round the man's thigh, Thomas managed to throw him off balance. As the fellow loosened his grip, Thomas wrenched the billet from his hand and banged it against the side of his head.

The man grunted and began to sag, air escaping from his mouth like a deflating bladder - then too late, Thomas heard something else whistle through the air behind him. It cracked down on the back of his skull with the force of a mallet. Perhaps it was a mallet, he thought vaguely, as he dropped to his knees with a singing in his ears, and lights floating before his eyes. Of course, there would be two of them... He was dimly aware of the big man struggling to his feet in front of him, fists working, and a pair of arms from behind hoisting him to his feet. Then he was held, pinioned, and the blows came thick and fast to his face, chest and stomach, and a blackness rolled down upon him. As he sank into unconsciousness, he thought he heard a distant shout, and running footsteps. Then there was nothing.

When he came awake minutes later, gasping for breath as if breaking the surface of a dark pond, he was lying in the dirt with an aching body and warm blood trickling down his face. Struggling to clear his blurred vision, he was startled to see a large man in ragged, patched clothes fighting with another man, not five yards away.

The ragged man, it seemed, had the upper hand. One of Thomas's two attackers, the one whom he had not seen, was rolling on the ground whimpering and clutching his head. The other, the beefy, red-faced one in the Spanish jerkin, was thrashing his arms about while the newcomer bore him downwards in some sort of wrestling hold. Little by little, the ragged man forced his opponent down, until with a cry the man fell on his knees, shouting for mercy.

The ragged man let go and stood panting, swinging his gaze from one ruffian to the other. The flabby man struggled to his feet, backing away, then kicked at his companion, who yelped and scrambled up, hands still pressed to his forehead. With an oath, the big man looked about for his club, which was lying a few feet away. But as he started towards it, the ragged man took a determined step, and the next second both bullies had turned tail and were running off down the alley, cursing and stumbling over the refuse. They rounded the corner and were gone.

Thomas had got himself to a sitting position. With his back to a wall, he sat breathing deeply and watched as the man in the patched clothes walked heavily towards him. It was then that he recognized him: the ex-soldier with the white scar running down his neck, into whose bowl he had dropped a groat on that first ride through the city, two days back. It already seemed a long time ago.

'Can you stand?' the man said, halting in front of him. He had not escaped the fray unscathed: there was a cut over his eye, and a large bruise forming on his cheek. He looked down at Thomas and frowned, as if trying to remember where he had seen him.

'I believe I can,' Thomas answered weakly. 'If my ribs don't fold in on me.'

The ex-soldier bent down, scanning Thomas's injuries with a keen eye. Then he stuck out a hand, and Thomas grasped it and allowed his rescuer to pull him to his feet.

'I'm in your debt, friend,' he said, wincing at the pain in his sides and stomach. The dizziness was beginning to clear.

'I saw those two follow you,' the other said. 'When you turned into the alley and one of them ducked into St George's Lane, I knew they were set to cut you off, one at each end.' He paused, looking hard at Thomas. 'They weren't after your purse, were they? Enemies of yours?'

Thomas did not reply. He felt foolish; he had been followed, of course - he was an easy mark, as he made his clumsy enquiries among the dealers. Had this beating been to warn him off, or something worse?

'I never saw them before,' he said finally. Then he added: 'But you, I have. Remember the well-mounted servant, who gave you a groat the other day, in Little Eastcheap?'

The man's eyes narrowed. 'I believe I do. You were riding behind a fine-dressed lady, and her maid.'

'I was,' Thomas said. 'And now I'll do better than drop a coin in your bowl. Can I buy you dinner, and all the ale you need to wash it down?'

The ragged man nodded, and a smile appeared. 'You can.'

'May I know your name?' Thomas asked. 'I'm Thomas Finbow, from Berkshire. I'm a falconer.' He offered a hand. After a moment, the other took it.

'Matthew Selden,' the ragged man said. 'I'm nought but a beggar.'

He spoke the word without shame. Thomas met his eyes and said: 'If I can do aught to change that, I will.'

Then, walking stiffly after their tussle, the two men picked their way out of the evil-smelling alleyway into the busy lane.

CHAPTER 8

Matthew Selden and Thomas sat at a table in a corner booth and ate hungrily. Though they had wiped the dirt from their clothes and the blood from their cuts, both still bore the look of prize fighters come straight from the fair. Perhaps, Thomas mused as he took a long drink of tepid ale, that was why nobody in the noisy, crowded ordinary gave them a second glance.

Selden wasted no time. He ate and drank enough for two men, then leaned back, the last piece of pippin pie still clutched in his large fist, and gave a contented sigh.

'Maybe you could have yourself assaulted more often, falconer. Then I'd get to eat regular.'

Thomas massaged his jaw, which was somewhat swollen. 'I was careless. Was a time I'd never have let myself get trimmed like that.'

Selden grimaced. 'With me, it's all of a piece. I've been living by my fists, or by my wits, since I was twelve years old.'

Thomas considered. 'I can speak to my lady. The mistress of the estate where I serve, in Berkshire. If she would find a place for you, are you willing?'

Selden seemed surprised. 'I thought that was just talk. Mayhap you're a man of his word.' He swallowed the last piece of pie and considered. 'I'd like to get off the streets. It's not worked out like I wanted it to.'

'Then let me try,' Thomas said. 'I owe you much - perhaps my life.'

Selden gave him a long look. 'Looks as if somebody must have a serious grudge against you.' When Thomas hesitated, he added: 'No matter - it's none of my business.'

'There's little I could tell, anyway,' Thomas said, with a feeling of helplessness. He gazed across the noisy room. Some men were smoking the new weed, tobacco, and a blue haze hung in the air. 'If I knew where to begin...' he stopped himself.

'I said it's naught of my affair,' Selden told him. 'But...'

Thomas turned sharply, nodding to him to continue.

'If I was wanting to seek out those two knaves, and pay them back in kind, I'd start on Bankside.' He took up his mug and drained it in one long pull.

Thomas stared. 'You know those men?'

Selden shook his head. 'But I've seen them. And if they run with the pack I think they do, I'd keep well away.'

'Why is that? Tell me.'

His tone was too urgent. Selden looked warily at him and said: 'I'm loath to become a part of another man's feud, falconer.'

'I wouldn't blame you for that,' Thomas answered. 'But I'd be grateful for any scrap of news you can throw me.'

Selden looked about him, then said in a low voice: 'I'd wager a day's money, they're part of Lynch's swarm.'

'Who's Lynch?' Thomas asked.

'John Lynch. A very bad fellow.'

'How? What is he?'

Selden snorted. 'There's no one word to describe such as he. I can tell you what he once was - a ruffler. A common beggar like me, only better dressed - tricked up like a cockerel. Pretended to being an ex-soldier, yet never left these shores, nor lifted pike or sword for his country. He used to tramp the roads of Middlesex with his doxy and his dell, till the girl grew old enough to spit in his eye and took off to fadge for herself.'

Intrigued, Thomas pressed his companion further; but Selden shrugged and said that it was common knowledge, among the masterless folk. When Thomas offered to call for more ale, the ragged man declined.

'You'll not loosen my tongue so easy as that, falconer.'

'I wouldn't think to,' Thomas answered. Then coming to a decision, he told Selden of the falcons.

The other man's frown deepened as he listened. Thomas finished by saying: 'You'll understand me now when I tell you I must follow the scent, no matter what the dangers, if it will lead me to the men who did that.'

Selden nodded. 'I can understand,' he said. 'But there's little more I can tell. Lynch left the vagrom life long ago, and took himself across the river. He's a thief and a crossbiter - uses a trull to set up some poor dupe, then takes his money. He's a pelting rogue who wouldn't scruple to slit your gizzard, falconer. And he's got a parcel of devils about him to do his bidding. That enough enemies for you?'

Thomas gazed into the bottom of his tankard. What in God's name, he thought, could such people have to do with Lady Margaret? It was absurd.

But if this was the trail, he must pursue it. 'Then, I must start looking on Bankside.'

'You'd be damned for a fool if you did,' Selden said. 'They know what you look like. You'll finish up in the river.'

That was true. In any case, he was not sure what to do, even if he found John Lynch. The

man could deny everything - what had he to do with falcons, or the ruffians who had attacked Thomas, or Lady Margaret, or with anything else?

With a sinking heart, Thomas considered his choices. He had always tried to live an honest life, yet he had little faith in the forces of law. In any case, Lady Margaret wanted secrecy. She had placed her trust in him. Here in London, he was a stranger. He felt he was being drawn, for reasons he barely understood, into a dark cavern with tunnels leading off in all directions. He was a man of the outdoors, of the open Downs and the sky. He would fail.

He shook himself out of his gloom and looked up to see Selden watching him closely.

'I trust few men, master falconer,' he said quietly, 'but you're probably one of them.'

Thomas said nothing.

'You've said you'll help me to a place. With a livery?'

Thomas nodded. 'If I can.'

'Then I'll help you, if I can.'

Suddenly Thomas remembered the gold earring. With hopes rising, he drew it out of his pocket. 'One of those who killed the birds - if there was more than one - lost this in the tussle. He'll have a torn ear, and maybe more cuts besides.'

Selden nodded. 'Any other signs?'

Another thought occurred. It was unlikely, but; 'You might try and discover whether any of Lynch's men can use a crossbow.'

Selden raised an eyebrow. 'Ex-soldier?'

'Could be.'

The ragged man got to his feet. 'I thank you for the dinner, Thomas Finbow.' Thomas stood up too, but Selden said: 'I'll leave alone, if it's all the same to you.'

Thomas nodded and sat down again. 'Where might I find you?'

'At the Black Bull, in Aldersgate Street.' He moved away. 'I make no promises to you.'

Thomas nodded and picked up his tankard. By the time he had put it down again and glanced about the room, Selden had gone.

When Thomas returned to the Brooke house it was late afternoon. He entered the kitchen to find everything in turmoil: Sir Marcus and Lady Alice had sent word that they were leaving Berkshire and returning to town the next day, earlier than anticipated.

He had no time to consider the implications of this news, because he was at once the object of attention. He had all but forgotten his appearance, until Jane Bull gave a cry.

'What has happened? You've been attacked!'

Embarrassed, he tried to dismiss the matter. The servants eyed him curiously, going about their duties in a hushed manner.

'You'll catch it when your mistress hears,' Jane said. 'Getting into fights - was it 'prentice boys mocking your country accent?'

'How did you know that?' Thomas asked, seizing the explanation.

'I hope you gave as good as you got,' Jane said. 'I've got some witch-hazel you can put on. Help the swelling go down.'

'Later, perhaps,' he said. 'First I must go to my lady.'

'Looking like that? You can't.'

'I have things to tell her.'

Jane clicked her tongue. 'Lady Alice would dismiss any of the men here, if they came before her in that state.'

'Lady Margaret wouldn't,' Thomas said. 'But I suppose I'd best tidy myself up.'

As he started to go, he felt a touch on his arm. Under her breath, Jane said: 'I must be wary, now my mistress is coming back.'

'I know it,' Thomas answered.

With a quick flick of her head, she moved away.

Lady Margaret gave instructions for Thomas to come to her the moment she heard of his return. She was taking an early supper in the banqueting hall, with only serving-men in attendance. As he walked in, he saw her at the far end of the huge table, a pale, delicate figure in a lilac-coloured dress. She was wearing jewels, too: rings, and a necklace of pearls set in silver.

He approached her awkwardly, the embrace of that morning seeming like a distant memory. She was the lady now, he but a servant; and one who was looking far from elegant. But she rose quickly from her chair and came towards him. As she drew closer, she stopped and put out a hand, then drew it back as if afraid.

'Thomas... what have I sent you into?'

He started to speak, but she turned abruptly and dismissed the servants. When they had gone she turned back to him, saying: 'No more. We will leave this matter. You have heard Sir Marcus and Lady Alice are returning tomorrow. I expect they will bring word from my husband, telling me to come home at once.'

She motioned him to a chair, but he shook his head. Matters were beyond him now. 'My

lady, I'm but your falconer,' he said, and tried to force a smile.

But she was not listening. 'I've been so very foolish... I've opened doors that should have remained shut. This path is dangerous for you, and I would not have you hurt.'

She looked about in agitation, making sure they were alone. The doors were all closed. She approached him then, and standing directly before him, placed a hand on his bruised cheek.

He longed to put his arms about her, but taking a long breath, he began instead to tell her of the events of the day. She lowered her head and moved towards the table. As he finished telling her of Selden, she went to one of the chairs and sank into it. Placing her hands on either side of her forehead, she said: 'I fear you will get naught for your pains but another beating - or worse. You must abandon this quest.'

He was silent for a moment. 'And the falcons, my lady?'

She considered. 'There are other dealers. We may make some enquiries...' Suddenly, she snapped out: 'This desire of my husband for a Norwegian falcon! It's nothing more than his vanity - a wish to keep as fine a flock of hawks as Sir Marcus!'

She looked up at Thomas. 'I am content with my merlin.'

She stood up beside the great table, saying: 'We'll return to Petbury. There are no gyrfalcons to be had, and the thought of Lady Alice's company for more than a few hours fills me with horror.'

At that, he tried not to laugh, but a snort escaped his lips. Looking quickly at him, she allowed herself a smile. 'You would like to be home again, would you not?'

He thought then of Eleanor, and nodded. The idea of leaving London and its dangers behind now seemed very attractive.

At that moment the door opened and the elderly serving-man entered. He bowed to Lady Margaret, threw a look of disapproval at Thomas, and said: 'My lady, there is a man asking to see you. A scholar of some sort, I believe.'

He waited. Lady Margaret waited too, then asked:

'Does he have a name?'

'John Pollard, my lady.'

There was a short silence, then she said: 'Ask him to come to the garden chamber. I will go there shortly.'

The man bowed. 'Does your ladyship wish for anything more?' He indicated the table,

where Lady Margaret's interrupted meal lay. She shook her head. 'I am no longer hungry.'

As the man left the room, she turned to Thomas and said:

'Once again, I ask you to be my witness.'

John Pollard wore the same threadbare suit in which he had always been seen at Petbury. He stood in the middle of the room looking as awkward and as mournful as ever, though if anything a little leaner. To Lady Margaret's polite enquiries about his present circumstances, he replied that he was now engaged as a tutor out at the village of Highgate. It was a family of modest means, but one such as he must be grateful for any sort of employment. As the atmosphere grew a little strained, he said: 'Lady Margaret, what I have come here to say is for your ears alone.'

'I wish Thomas to remain,' Lady Margaret said.

But unlike Nicholas Stocker the day before, Pollard was adamant. The matter was delicate, he dared not broach it in the presence of anyone else, not even a trusted servant like the falconer.

She frowned. She had never liked Pollard very much, though she had not the same antipathy towards him that her husband did. As she weighed the man's words, Thomas grew tense. He recalled his last encounter with the tutor, at the party after Nathaniel's funeral.

The silence grew longer. He saw Lady Margaret throw him a glance, and said: 'My lady, mayhap I should go about my duties.'

She nodded. 'I will consider what is to be done - about the falcons,' she added, as if it were some everyday business that would naturally concern him.

He bowed and, with a brief nod at Pollard, who stood rigid as a fence-post, left the room, closing the door behind him.

For want of something to occupy him, he went to the stables and found James feeding the horses. The animals stamped in their stalls, munching contentedly on hay and bran. These were more the sort of surroundings that suited Thomas. He greeted the young groom, who looked up at him, glanced at his bruised face and turned quickly away.

'I heard you'd got yourself into a bit of trouble.'

'It could have been a deal worse,' Thomas said, and walked to where Lady Margaret's mare stood. He stroked the animal's neck, murmuring a few soft words.

'Find out anything more?' James asked. 'About the killing?'

Thomas shook his head. He had no desire to involve James further in the matter - or anyone

else now.

'There's some dark business there, isn't there?' James muttered, filling a pail from a sack of oats that stood against the wall.

Thomas shrugged. 'I don't know where to start looking. I'm but a countryman.'

James threw him a sly look. 'Nothing wrong with country folk.' He paused, then added: 'Take her ladyship's maid, now.'

Thomas broke into a broad smile. One thing at least, had suddenly become clear to him. 'You've been chasing after Catherine.'

'No I haven't,' James grinned. 'But the way she acts, I don't believe she'd mind if I did.'

'Well,' Thomas replied, 'I'm sorry to bear bad news, but I think we'll be leaving in the next day or so.'

James's face fell. 'I thought Lady Vicary had business to see to.'

'It's all but finished,' Thomas said, and turned to go, then stopped dead. He had remembered Matthew Selden, who might be putting himself in danger this very evening, ferreting about in the taverns, the gaming-houses and stews, and all the myriad haunts of the underworld.

James's thoughts were elsewhere, now that it seemed Catherine was about to leave him. As Thomas turned to go out, there was the sound of footsteps hurrying across the cobbled yard, and Catherine herself appeared in the doorway.

'Thomas,' she began, a little out of breath, 'the mistress wants you at once...' Then seeing James she stopped dead, and her cheeks flushed pink. Thomas stepped aside to let her enter the stable, then with a smile at the two of them, went back to the house.

He went immediately to the room where he had left Lady Margaret and found her alone, standing by the window. Outside the light was fading; candles were being carried about the house. Though there was a fire in the room, she was shaking.

She signalled for him to draw close. Quickly she said: 'Thomas, we cannot go yet. Things are gone more awry than I thought... I am facing my ruin.'

He stood helplessly and watched her fighting back tears. He knew now that he loved her, as surely as he knew she was beyond his reach.

CHAPTER 9

When Thomas went to his bed that night he made no attempt to go to sleep. When faced with a puzzle it was his habit to try looking at the terrain from afar, as a soaring hawk might view it; and now it seemed to grow into focus.

Lady Margaret had not told him all; but as he knew more about John Pollard than she realized, it was not too difficult for him to form a picture. Pollard was probably aware of Nathaniel Pickering's desires, because he shared such feelings himself. It was clear that he had borne a hopeless love for young William Vicary who, Thomas guessed, would have played upon it: he was a crafty and manipulative boy. Had Pollard tried to tell Lady Margaret that her son was of the same sexual persuasion? Thomas knew that was not true - as any of the prettier scullery-maids and farmer's daughters around Petbury could testify. No: Pollard must have some other hold over Lady Margaret to have caused her such distress. Perhaps he had learned something more important from Nathaniel; something touching on her family.

Pollard knew things that would harm her. Lonely, bitter and short of money, he had come to ask her to buy his silence. Whether she had agreed or not, she was now resolved. She had to find the enemies that threatened her - for she was in some real danger, he knew: he had the injuries done to his own person to testify to it. And it had not been without some unease that he had promised to keep searching. They would stay in London for another three days; his mistress would have to suffer Lady Alice's company after all.

No matter how he tried to put aside his own feelings for her, he knew that he would risk any danger to bring her peace. Then they might return to their own fair county, and leave this noisome city behind. Exhausted by the day's events, he fell at last into a deep sleep. The other men did not wake him at dawn, but rose and went about their work. So, it was in the mid-morning of a crisp, sunny autumn day when Thomas awoke refreshed, and determined on his course. He was the hawk, yet his quarry was the stronger, and he was outnumbered.

While Lady Margaret prepared to receive Sir Marcus and Lady Brooke, Thomas left the house and made his way from the Strand to Fleet Street. He had asked James for directions, and a rough map of the city's environs was beginning to form in his mind. Turning to the left before Ludgate on this Friday morning, he skirted the city walls, walked along Old Bailey into Giltspur Street and entered the maze of houses and shops that clustered about Pie Corner and West Smithfield. Threading a way through narrow streets and their by-now-familiar stink of refuse, through the throng of servants and townswomen doing their shopping, the barking dogs and the sick and lame about St Bartholomew's Hospital, he emerged by Little Britain

and turned left into Aldersgate Street. Some way along, he found the notorious Black Bull Inn, and stepped inside.

At first, he saw little because the place was dark and smoky, even at this hour. It smelled of stale beer and wine, sweat and tobacco. Gradually he made out figures seated at tables, some of whom glanced at him as he eased his way through. A drawer in a dirty leather apron appeared abruptly and asked what he wanted. Calling for a glass of sack, he found a stool at the end of a scarred table and sat himself down. It was then, with relief, that he saw Matthew Selden, sitting on a bench against the far wall with a tankard in his fist. As Thomas's eyes met his, the ex-soldier looked away quickly and began talking intently to the fellow next to him. This was how it would be: he must pretend not to know the man.

For the best part of an hour he sat with his glass of poor sack, trying to look like a casual drinker with time on his hands, while rough men came and went, sometimes brushing against Thomas with undisguised hostility. Had he chosen to challenge any one of them, he would have had a fight on his hands, the day after his painful encounter in the alley by Pudding Lane. Tiring of the place and of the company, he drained his glass and was about to leave when he saw Selden get up from the far table, clap one or two fellows on the shoulder in farewell and make his way to the door without looking in Thomas's direction. After a moment, Thomas rose and followed him outside.

Looking to right and left, he caught sight of the patched clothes of his new friend moving off up Aldersgate Street, away from the city. He followed, until the walls were far behind and the fields were all about them, and birdsong replaced the cries and shouts of London. The road led uphill towards the village of Islington, but long before that Selden, who had never looked back, turned right on to a grassy track below a low hill on which a windmill stood. When Thomas reached the spot, he saw the ex-soldier sitting with his back against a tree-stump, like any traveller who has stopped to rest in the sunshine.

'Seat yourself, falconer,' he said. 'The air here's sweeter than the tavern, is it not? I thought you'd prefer it.'

Thomas sat down, saying: 'I thought you would never leave that foul den.'

'You wouldn't want me to go before I'd gleaned all there was, would you?'

'You've made a discovery?'

'I have. Some pieces last night, in Blackfriars, that didn't hold well together, and a little more since that helped cement them - into a shape I like not.' The ex-soldier fumbled in his

pocket and pulled out a dirty clay pipe with a chipped bowl. It was stuffed with dark tobacco.

'Do you take the weed?' he asked.

Thomas shook his head. Selden found a worn tinder-box and struggled for some minutes to light the pipe. Finally, Thomas helped him light a dry twig, which he held in the bowl, sucking furiously, until the damp tobacco glowed unwillingly into life. Leaning back contentedly, Selden blew out a long stream of smoke.

'Your trail has winds and turns I can't follow, Master Thomas,' he said finally. 'I have neither means nor inclination to seek much further.'

'Whatever you've learned, I'm grateful for it,' Thomas replied.

'I wouldn't be, if I were you,' Selden said. 'You may be meddling in things above you. The gentry will tend to matters touching their own class.'

Thomas stared across the fields, where horses grazed in the sunshine. Here, less than a mile from London, was a different world, a lot closer to the one he knew. He waited for Selden to speak; the ragged man did not like to be hurried.

'I told you John Lynch has a daughter, did I not?' the other began. 'That he and his doxy kept about them when they walked the roads? A kinchin mort; a beggar's girl-child, good for drawing sympathy. She was - and is still, I hear - of rare beauty. Dark-eyed and dark-complexioned, with shiny black hair and a skin smooth as silk. Such a prize, that men have paid five guineas for a night with her.'

'She's a drab?'

'What else should she be, with her history?' Selden answered. 'She'd have been brought to the Upright Man at twelve years of age - he has a right to take any beggar's child when she's grown enough, and pinked. Broken for use, like a workhorse, falconer. Not pretty, is it.'

'No,' Thomas agreed. 'But what is she to my quest?'

'It's a plot fit for the theatre, across the fields there,' Selden continued, waving his pipe eastwards in the direction of Finsbury. 'See if I can piece it out for you.'

He took a lungful of tobacco, and went on: 'We go back, about eight years. The girl's name, is Susanna. She's fiery as a marten, and soon as she can, she leaves her father and his doxy - who isn't her mother, as anyone could see - reaches London, and takes herself across the river to the Stews, where there's ready work for such as she. There she serves her prenticeship and learns her trade, and rises above the plain flocks of Winchester Geese, because of her fine

looks. She becomes a celebrated woman - no cheap callet, for any man to fumble, but the best of the house, tricked out in rings and bobbets, a velvet gown and starched ruff - the plaything of those with gold in their purses instead of silver. She can pick and choose whom she beds – from the sons of yeomen, she rises to young gentlemen, thence to knights and earls. Within a few years, Susanna Lynch is the envy of the Bankside, and not poxed either - she treats herself like a lady, washes her body in white wine, and scents it with rosewater. How she's grown, eh falconer, from beggar-child to rich man's courtesan?'

Thomas listened, carried along by the ragged man's story. He had begun to wonder at its end, when Selden, puffing at his pipe, continued: 'And such a prize was bound to be picked up, plucked from the mire where she dwelled, and set in a garden where a certain rich man may visit her when he pleases, for his sport. She's closeted so they tell, in a fair house in Houndsditch, without the east wall, where she dwells in comfort with her own servant, like the lady she always wanted to be. Though she's a painted trull when all's said and done, and earns her bread on her back same as her sisters back in the Stews.'

Selden's pipe had gone out. He peered at it, then tossed it away. 'Now the story takes an odd twist, falconer. It seems Lynch, who's by now left the road and earning his living in Southwark by worse means than begging, learns of his daughter's new station, and where she dwells, and takes himself over there stoked up with liquid courage, to demand a share of her good fortune. Imagine the whoreson javel's anguish, when she flings a few pennies at him along with a stream of curses, and has her servant throw him out on his arse.'

He smiled a little at this. Then more softly, he added: 'But Lynch isn't done yet. He forces his way back into the house and starts shouting, and soon she's white as a wand. And after he's gone, she's shaking like a willow.'

He stopped then. Questions rose to Thomas's lips, but Selden shook his head as if in warning. 'We're close to the end of it, falconer. Lynch's girl says she won't receive him again, but what's passed between them has set something off... lit a fuse, that burns still for aught I know. Lynch has put his own plans in motion, to what end I know not. But you and your mistress, it appears to me, have figured in them. The ones who caught you in the alley are Lynch's people, that's certain.'

Thomas found that his mouth had become dry as tinder. He swallowed and asked: 'And the crossbow?'

Selden shrugged. 'There's true ex-soldiers he might call upon, not counterfeit ones like he. And other men, that are his eyes and ears. One's a Welshman called Laughing Morgan, wanders about feigning madness.'

Thomas turned sharply. 'Does he wear a yellow coat?'

Selden nodded, and frowned slightly. 'You're in the way of it, falconer. Hear this from me:

leave it all behind you, go back to your Berkshire Downs. There's naught but a poniard's point awaits you, if you delve deeper into Lynch's business.'

'But the girl...' Thomas searched for some meaning to it all.

Selden put out a hand unexpectedly and gripped his arm. 'There's the greatest danger. They say she belongs to a lord, one of the highest in the land. He'd swat such as you like a fly, if you strayed into his path. Leave it alone, falconer. Remember, it takes little to have a plain man clapped in prison. Once he's been there long enough, he's forgotten; by the time he goes free - if he ever does - he's old and broken, fit for naught but to beg scraps in the market.'

There was a silence. Thomas looked up into the sky, and watched the red kites wheel overhead, scattering starlings and sparrows before them. Higher, much higher, a heron flew in a straight course, bound for Hackney marshes. He thought suddenly of the falcons.

'Did you learn of a man who'd had his earring torn off?'

Selden shook his head.

'I know not what to do,' Thomas said, at last.

Selden grunted. 'There's only one course for you: leave the game, and go home.'

He got stiffly to his feet and looked down at Thomas, not unkindly. 'I'll give you farewell now. I've a living to make.'

Thomas got up too. 'I've yet to speak of you to my mistress, about a place. I planned to do it Sunday, after prayers.'

But Selden shook his head. 'I drank you, falconer, but it's not to be. I've grown used to the road. Best follow the ways I know.'

Thomas put out a hand as if to stay him. 'I swore to help you, as you have me.'

'You bought me a good dinner,' Selden said. 'It was a fair bargain.'

'Then, are we not to meet again?'

Selden shrugged. 'I'll not be at the Black Bull again for a long while. I stand out too much, less I get myself some new clothes.'

Thomas untied his purse from his belt and held it out. 'Take it. I'll brook no argument.'

After a moment, Selden took the purse. Then he held out a hand, and Thomas shook it.

Their hands closed in a strong grip.

'If you ever travel west beyond Newbury,' Thomas said, 'take the Wantage road northwards, then make for the Downs by Chaddleworth, and ask for the manor of Petbury. I'll see you're not turned away.'

Selden nodded, gave a half-smile, then turned and began walking at a steady pace back

towards London.

Thomas walked back slowly around the outskirts of the city, so deep in thought that he lost his way twice and had to ask directions. When he finally returned to Sir Marcus's house in the mid-afternoon, he found the master himself and Lady Alice had already arrived. Upon entering the kitchen, he was immediately told that Sir Marcus, Lady Alice and Lady Margaret would go hawking tomorrow at Pinnesnoll Hill near Muswell, as guests of the Earl of Stafford, and Thomas was to wait upon them.

The news cheered him. Not only would he at last be able to do the sort of work he knew, he might also have the opportunity for a moment's talk with Lady Margaret. He had resolved to try and persuade her to return to Petbury, and to leave behind the unwholesome business of her enquiries.

At the supper table, great events such as the trial of the Queen of Scots were forgotten; the servants' talk was all of Lady Alice's temper. The woman was at a difficult age, someone remarked, prompting giggles from the younger serving-maids. None dared voice the rumour already current: that Sir Marcus spent many nights away when he was in town, taking his pleasures elsewhere.

As everyone was rising to go about their evening duties, Catherine said to Thomas: 'That lawyer came again to see my lady. The fellow with the bald pate that was waiting at the old house, the day we arrived.'

Thomas paused. 'Did he tarry long with her?'

'No more 'n a few minutes.' Then lowering her voice, the girl muttered: 'You won't say nothing to her about me and James, will you?'

He smiled and shook his head.

The following day Thomas rode behind Lady Margaret, Sir Marcus Brooke and Lady Alice to the north of the city, beyond Islington and Highgate to the fair hills of Finchley. Here, aristocratic members of the London population had for years been building pleasant villas and even great mansions, far from the smoke and smells of the burgeoning capital. Among

these was the Earl of Stafford, an old friend to Sir Marcus, elderly but still a sporting man, with a fine stable of hawks and hounds. His sons and their ladies, with various friends, made up the large party which gathered on Pinnesnoll Hill by Muswell village. A wind blew from the west, but the Earl was in the mood for showing off his favourite hawk, a rebellious bird named Titus. His falconer, Jack Roker, had a cadge - a frame of poles pegged to the ground - whereon the hooded hawks were perched. He and Thomas were soon busy threading jesses

and varvels, handing birds up to the gentry who chatted on horseback and waited for the dogs to be brought up. Grouse and partridges were expected, along with pheasants and rabbits.

Roker was an Astringer, a skilled trainer of short-winged or 'true hawks' like goshawks and sparrowhawks. He and Thomas would have had much to talk of, but there was little time for conversation as the dogs sprang from their leashes and began to flush out the game. Sir Marcus, having no falcons at his London house, had the loan of a fine hawk of the Earl's, and was in excellent humour as he held it high and let it soar aloft, almost to the clouds.

Thomas had seen little of Lady Margaret. She rode with the ladies, carrying their smaller lanner falcons, hobbies and sakers. As the morning wore on and the hawking party moved further out across the hills, he had more than enough to do tending to the birds and bagging up their kill. Then during a lull in the activity he heard a tinkling of bells, and turned to see his mistress riding towards him with a hooded lanner falcon on her hand. Reining her mount, she said: 'I miss my Melisande.'

He smiled. 'I miss all the Petbury birds, my lady. I dare to think they in their turn have missed me.'

She gave a twitch on the rein and walked her horse forward until she and Thomas were close. As he took a step towards her, she leaned down to offer the falcon to him. He took it on to his own gauntlet, saying 'I have learned more of our - the business we spoke about.'

She glanced about to make sure that none of the party were in earshot, and said: 'Tell me now, quickly.'

He told her, as concisely as he was able, all that Selden had told him.

He wanted to add a word of his own, about Pollard, but was abashed by the look which came into her eyes. Clutching at the rein of her horse, which stirred restlessly, she said in agitated tones: 'I have learned a little more myself. Or rather, I have deduced more than I was told.'

She watched him place the bird on a bar of the cadge, and went on: 'Stocker presumes to warn me that my reputation is at stake; and that there are people who wish me ill.'

He stood up then and faced her, saying urgently: 'My lady, I beg you - let us return home. There are entanglements here that are beyond my skills or station. I know not the cause of these threats to you, but they are real, I am certain of it. This man Lynch, is a—'

'I know!' she cut in sharply. 'I see what he is. I must discover what he wants.'

'But why?' he asked, emboldened by her distress. He had to stop himself from reaching out to touch her. But she barely looked at him. There was some anguish that made her keep her

distance.

From a hundred yards away, shouts came. The party were moving back towards them, and Jack Roker was signalling to Thomas. He raised his hand in reply and looked to Lady Margaret, but she was already turning her horse. Before riding off, she leaned down to pat the mare's neck, so that their faces were level, and said: 'I will be alone in my room tonight. Wait until the house is quiet, then wait another hour, and come to me. The door will not be locked.'

Then with uncharacteristic force, she dug her heels into the mare's flanks, and sprang away

across the grass.

CHAPTER 10

He went as she had asked, or commanded, it almost seemed, for despite the foolhardiness of such an action, he had neither the will nor the inclination to stop himself.

The house was quiet - too quiet for his liking - as he crept in his stockinged feet up the back stairs, along the passage to Lady Margaret's door. No light was visible. He hesitated, wondering how she had got Catherine out of the way, then tapped gently on the door. At once it swung open, and before him was the dim figure of his mistress standing in her shift. As he stepped inside she closed the door behind him; they were alone together, in her chamber.

Now he was silent. If he had imagined such a scene, it was in a dream that was half-remembered, and bound up with a degree of anxiety and guilt. He was but her falconer, he told himself for the twentieth time - more accurately, he was her husband's falconer. Such trysts as this took place across the otherwise unbridgeable gulf of class, it was true, but only to other folk; the subject of salacious gossip in the servants' hall. Now, it was happening to him. There they stood in the gloom, barely a foot apart. With a throat as dry as dust he made an attempt at speech, but she put out a hand and pressed it to his mouth.

'This must happen only once,' she said in a whisper. 'You may know me, tonight, here in Sir Marcus's house. It will not be possible at Petbury.'

He swallowed, and sensed rather than saw her faint smile in the dark. 'I know who and what you are,' she went on, 'and what I do. I would not endanger you for the world and all its wealth. I will tell you...' she took a deep breath. 'You will understand me better, perhaps, if I tell you after we have been close - close as man and woman may be.'

'Catherine...' he began vaguely, but at once she said:

'Catherine is tumbling in the stable with her bold young groom, if I'm not mistaken.' Then she added: 'We are mistress and servant, but we are also two women who share a chamber.'

He brought his hands up to her face, and held it gently. She gave a sigh, and leaned forward. This time, when their lips touched in the dark, it was the start of a lingering kiss filled with promise. Though he thought briefly of Jane Bull down the corridor, it was merely a fleeting memory that was gone, as he folded the tall slim woman into his arms and gave himself up to her body. And when she backed towards the huge bed, drawing him with her through the gossamer curtains, he thought suddenly of a day long ago, when as a boy of fourteen or fifteen, running with the other village lads on a baking hot summer's day, he had thrown off his clothes and waded into a pool in the Petbury woods, letting himself sink blissfully under the water until it closed over his head. He believed at that moment, that he

cared not if he never came up again.

In the dead time of night, with no sound from beyond the casement but an occasional owl hoot, they lay between her sweat-soaked sheets, arms wrapped about each other. She was Lady Margaret still, but she was another Lady Margaret now: one that he would never be able to forget. The thought alarmed him, as he considered the future that lay ahead.

But she talked, and he listened, and understood now that there was no one else in whom she dared confide. Her husband...? Sir Robert was a memory, far away, and she was here with him clutching his hand, her head on his chest.

'I take after my father,' she said. 'I was a wayward child, curious about things outside and far off... roaming the lanes, and the fields outside the city, and getting lost and being brought home to be scolded. But he couldn't stay angry at me: he knew we were of the same spirit. The one that made him seek after knowledge and follow paths lesser men feared to tread.'

She was quiet, remembering. Her breath rose and fell on his bare chest. In the distance, he heard what sounded like the booming of a bittern from somewhere upriver.

'He befriended men of science like himself. He was eager for news the explorers brought back, from Africa, the Americas... He might have gone with Martin Frobisher to seek for the passage through the ice, had he lived.'

Her voice fell, so low that he could barely hear. 'It was shame that killed him. My shame, and the cruelty of my brother.'

He was eager to know her story, but held back. She would tell it in her own way.

She shuddered. 'I had a child, Thomas. Before I was married.'

He knew it - suddenly, it seemed that he had always known it. It explained her loveless marriage, the sadness that no one could account for. It explained why she had told him, but an hour ago, that he would understand better after they had coupled. She was a hot and passionate woman beneath a cool exterior which he, at least, had always known was false. In the dark he squeezed her hand, silently urging her to continue.

'I had a child - but that child could not be allowed to live, because of its...' she almost sobbed. 'Because of the father.'

He stroked her hair, and asked gently: 'Who was he?'

She was silent. He waited, but there was only her breathing, more controlled now. Finally, she said: 'The child is gone, and I was married off to a rich knight, and have borne him two fair children of his own. I must make what I can, of such cloth as I have.'

Afraid she would say no more, he pressed her with questions. 'Did your brother threaten to

tell Sir Robert?'

She gave a slight nod. 'Nathaniel had neither shame nor pity, save in the matter of the scandal that would come upon our family, and so damage his feeble prospects. He persuaded my father the child must be taken from me, all those years ago.'

He frowned. He saw how she had indeed been spared some pain by her brother's death. But there was more; he burned to know all.

'The secret is known to others,' he ventured. 'John Pollard, perhaps?'

She gave a tiny sniff of contempt. 'He knows a little, and guessed a little more - he's a poor hand at blackmail compared to my brother.'

'Then what is your fear?'

She gripped his hand then, tighter than before, and answered: 'I dare not tell even you. You may not understand.'

'I would try as hard as I might.'

'Even so...' she seemed tired, suddenly. 'It is old history. The threat that has burst upon me - upon us both, stems from some darker motive... I dread to look far into it.'

'Yet, you urged me to find out what I could.'

'Yes.' She sighed. 'To find out who they are, then I might know how to deal with them, without my husband finding out.'

'Why did they want to kill your brother?' he asked.

'Why did one come to my window and knock, without attempting to enter?' she countered. Then in a different tone, she added: 'If my husband learns all I would be ruined, Thomas, have no doubts of that. Already he has sent word by Sir Marcus that he is angry at my having stayed away so long without sending him news. He is coming here in two days, to fetch me home.'

He was silent. Though he felt some relief at the news it was tinged with fear, for her sake. She went on: 'If he knew all, I would be as a condemned woman - an outcast, or worse. He would scorn me - they all would. Perhaps even you.'

'You must not believe that,' he whispered, and tightened his arm about her. 'Whatever you have done, I would not turn from you.'

She raised her head then, and kissed him on the mouth. 'My dear, gentle falconer. Would we had been born of the same station, I would have cleaved to you and borne your children,

and asked for nothing more than to have you beside me at night.'

She slid her hand across his chest, murmuring softly: 'We have but a few hours before

dawn. Do not waste them.'

On Sunday morning, while the household stood at prayers, several pairs of eyes peered conspiratorially about the chapel from under half-lowered lids. Catherine's eyes met those of James the groom, and a look of joyful contentment passed between them. Jane Bull's eyes sought those of Thomas, and found them not on hers, but gazing forward to the carved oaken pews of the gentry, where Lady Margaret stood with head bowed beside Lady Alice and her husband. Lady Margaret's eyes looked down at the paved floor, then strayed across it to the stained-glass windows beyond.

Sir Marcus, his wife and Lady Margaret filed out with the servants following. Thomas emerged into the cloudy morning to see Lady Margaret some way ahead, walking tight-lipped and pale beside a frowning Lady Alice. All did not look well; he suspected their hosts had not been pleased to learn of the events of the last few days. When they reached the house, and Lady Margaret sent for Thomas at once, he learned the worst.

She sat in the morning-room as before, but this time Lady Alice was there too. As Thomas entered, she snapped: 'I wish to know why you have done naught to inform the city authorities about the slaughter of the gyrfalcons.'

He stood stiffly before her and said: 'I have tried to discover the culprits myself, my lady. It has proved difficult.'

She snorted like a Flanders mare. She was a short, solid woman, made even bulkier by her elaborate farthingale. She continued: 'Sir Marcus is displeased, falconer, as I am - and we are both greatly alarmed by the report of intruders in the garden. Such a coil has never happened here. You were entrusted with Lady Margaret's safety, in the place of her steward. You should have taken steps to protect her.'

'He has done so,' Lady Margaret said quietly, but her hostess was in no mood to be interrupted. With a frown, she continued: 'As for the birds - a most wicked, unspeakable crime - as I understand your mistress had already paid for them, it was a crime against her property; for which you, as falconer, were responsible. Is that not so?'

'I believe your ladyship is correct,' he answered.

'Then what steps do you propose to take, to remedy it?'

'Lady Alice,' Lady Margaret's cool voice interjected. 'I beg to remind you that my falcons,

and my falconer, are my concern, and that of my husband. It is for him to decide what steps are to be taken, if any.'

Lady Alice's fleshy lips parted in a sickly smile. 'Of course, my duck. As you wish.' She

turned towards Thomas, but the rebuke seemed to be addressed more to Lady Margaret.

'Today is the sabbath; you are free to go. However, as you are aware, preparations must be made for your return to Berkshire. I trust you will employ the time more diligently than you have thus far. I will speak to Sir Robert about your conduct, which I find somewhat proud, and inattentive.'

She turned to Lady Margaret. 'Have you anything to add, madam?'

Lady Margaret gave a slight shake of her head. Lady Alice stared coldly at Thomas, leaving him in no doubt that the interview was concluded. As he gave a short bow, though he tried hard to stop himself he caught Lady Margaret's eye, and saw her desperation.

She implored his help, still. With a heavy heart he turned to leave the chamber, wondering what he might possibly do in the one day that remained.

Needing to collect his thoughts, he went directly to the stables and found James, who was in a mood of high excitement. After making sure no one was about the yard, the groom closed the door and pulled a bottle out from under a pile of hay.

'Join me in a drink of celebration, Thomas,' he said, and took a pull. 'Catherine's going to ask your ladyship to ask Lady Alice if I can leave service here - and go with you to Berkshire!'

He handed Thomas the bottle. Thomas raised it to him and drank. 'I wish you luck,' he said. 'But I wouldn't set my hopes too high. I don't believe Lady Alice is well disposed towards any of us this morning.'

'Oh, that's always her way.' James brushed it aside and took another drink. 'She'll cool herself. Then me and Catherine can be wedded!'

The young man looked so happy that Thomas had not the heart to dampen his spirits. He joined him and his cheap wine, sitting beside him on a bale of straw. Both fell silent; each man's thoughts, had he spoken them, would have been remarkably similar. They dealt with the activity of the previous night, and the female company that had occasioned it.

As Thomas sat watching the horses in their stalls, a resolve began to form. There were few paths to choose from. Perhaps he should go back into the city, and try to find Selden?

But then, he almost snorted at his own foolishness; proverbs about needles and haystacks

sprang to mind. In any case, the ragged man would not have pressed his enquiries further.

He considered his possible sources of aid or information. Pollard? He was unlikely to be of much help. Stocker? The lawyer would tell him nothing, and probably make more trouble in his turn. Then he remembered the Dutchman, van Velsen. If he was close to finding the ones

who killed the falcons, he believed the dealer might come to his aid, if only out of vengeance. Might that not be a place to start?

He stood up, stretched himself, and saw James watching him with a sly look. A flicker of alarm must have crossed his face, for the groom winked and said: 'Fear not falconer, your secret's safe in my hands. We're of one mind, are we not?'

Thomas froze, but the next moment relief flooded over him when James added: 'You and mistress Jane. Don't try and cozen me!'

Allowing a grin to appear, Thomas said: 'If you need a friend when you get to Petbury, I'd be obliged for your silence now, on that matter.'

James waved the bottle at him. 'No more to be said. I'm your friend, Thomas. Always will be.'

Thomas clapped him lightly on the shoulder and went out. Within the hour he had passed through the city walls by Ludgate, turned right down St Andrew's Hill and was walking briskly the entire length of Thames Street, parallel to the river. A light rain began to fall. The streets were quiet except near the churches, where crowds gathered and bells rang the noon hour. It was pleasant to walk, even through the mire and refuse that lay everywhere. He maintained his pace through the Keys, almost deserted at this hour, until he found himself at the entrance to Botolph, and turned down it to the Dutchman's.

The shop was closed and shuttered, but he expected that like most traders the man would live on the premises. Thomas knocked loudly on the doors and peered up at the windows of the upper storey, but there was no answer.

Fighting his disappointment, he was about to turn away when a door opened in the next shop and the round face of the wool dealer appeared: the one who had laughed at him when he made his enquiries, three days back. With a mouth full of dinner, the man mumbled: 'There's nobody in. This hour of a Sunday, you'll find all such as him at the Dutch church.'

'Where is that?' Thomas asked, standing in the rain, whereupon the dealer recognized him and said: 'You're the fellow that was asking about the dead falcons.'

Thomas nodded.

The man swallowed, wiped his mouth and said: 'The Dutch church is next to the French church.' Then as a pained look spread across

Thomas's features he added with a smile. 'A jest, friend. I know you're a stranger to the town. Walk northwards by Gracious Street and Cornhill, then by the Exchange into Three Needle, which gives to the right on to Broad Street. There you may find the Dutch church, in the old Austin Friars.'

Thomas thanked him and walked off. Briskly, he crossed Thames Street and tramped the length of Botolph Lane, intending to ask directions to Gracious Street. As he emerged into Little Eastcheap, where a few people passed to and fro, he paused and looked about, recalling his first journey through here, and his encounter with Selden. Today there was no market, nor any row of beggars spread out along it in their various guises. Or rather there was just one: an odd-looking fellow in a bright yellow coat, with bare arms and long reddish hair that hung wet about his face. He was standing on the other side of the street, on the corner of Philpot Lane, swaying from side to side and wearing what seemed to Thomas a false, if permanent, grin.

Thomas came to a dead halt and spun to the right in the direction of Tower Street, staring down at his wet boots. His heart thudding, he slowed after a few steps and risked a quick glance behind. The Abraham man did not appear to have observed him. He stood with a begging bowl in his hand, rattling it at passers-by. Now, the sound of his laughter reached Thomas's ears: a manic cackle, honed to chilling perfection by years of practice.

Unwittingly, he had found Laughing Morgan; but what, now, was he to do with him?

CHAPTER 11

He waited, sheltering from the rain that now poured steadily, under eaves and any other overhang that offered itself, so long as he was able to keep the laughing beggar in sight. He tried to take special care that he in turn was not spotted, for at no time was he fooled by the vacant, unseeing expression on the fellow's face. Though he was twenty yards away he believed he could see a pair of greenish eyes, sharp as a goshawk's, peering up and down the street from under the fringe of dirty hair that was plastered to the man's forehead.

He had resolved to follow him, if it took the rest of the day. After dark he knew the city gates would be shut, which would make things difficult; perhaps he could make his way home by the river. For he dared not be found absent by morning, on the day his master was due to arrive. That would raise more questions than he could hope to answer.

After an hour Laughing Morgan swung himself about and moved off up Philpot Lane, turning left into Fenchurch Street. Ahead was the crossroads where Gracious Street intersected with Lombard Street beyond. The beggar had a shambling walk that, Thomas soon realized, deceived the eye in the speed with which he covered the ground. As he followed the man across into Lombard Street he had to quicken his pace a little, passing St Clement's Lane and St Nicholas's Lane, with the church bells clanging in disharmony. People crossed from Abchurch towards Cornhill and back, and on some occasions, dodging through them, he lost sight of his quarry. Each time he saw him again he breathed a grateful thanks, for the man's bright yellow coat would have stood out not merely in a midden, as one of Sir Marcus's maids had said, but in a field of sunflowers.

Then he lost him.

At first, he assumed the beggar had turned left by the churchyard of St Laurence Poultriey. Hurrying around it, he looked down every opening, fetching up in St Swithin's Lane, but saw no trace of a yellow coat. Almost breaking into a run, he walked back into Lombard Street, turned left and hurried on until the way opened into a broad avenue, with Cornhill on his right and Three Needle Street beyond. Here was the Stocks Market, at the very heart of London, where on any other day the throng would have been so great, it would have been difficult to follow anyone. Today the crowds were sparse, but still he had not been able to spot a bright yellow coat on a grey afternoon. He cursed himself for a fool, looking in all directions; then he froze.

Laughing Morgan was standing less than ten yards away, cackling, at the entrance to Cornhill. He must have ducked into a passage on the right, then doubled back along the

narrow way known as the Cardinal's Hat, to end up behind him. Was he letting Thomas know that he was aware of being followed?

He had no choice but to take that chance. Determined not to let the man out of his sight again for one moment, Thomas crossed the square and turned right into Three Needle Street, then walking as fast as he dared, cut right again as soon as he was able, to emerge in the broad street of Cornhill by the Tun. On his left, the palatial Royal Exchange towered above him, but he had no time to admire the fair sights of London. With relief he saw Laughing Morgan's yellow coat once again and took up a position in a doorway from where he could observe at leisure.

The chase continued all afternoon. Cold, wet and hungry, Thomas dogged the footsteps of the laughing beggar, towards whom he was developing a feeling of intense animosity. After some time, he began to see that there was a pattern to the man's movements. He would beg for an hour or so at a particular spot, a corner where the crowds were greatest, particularly near the churches. Many a charitable soul, coming fresh from a sermon, dipped into purse or pocket to lay coins in the man's bowl. Watching keenly, Thomas saw him use the old gambit of emptying the bowl into some hidden fold of his coat while no one was looking, leaving only a few farthings, before moving on to his next station. That way was best, for arousing sympathy.

As the light began to dim, Thomas realized that he might soon be caught in the city with nowhere to stay and have to explain his presence to the watch. As he pondered the situation, his eyes bleared with the effort of fixing on Laughing Morgan, he saw the man move off again. By now quarry and stalker had worked their way westwards across the city to St Paul's, where crowds were beginning to congregate for evensong. Here, at any hour of the day, a great number of beggars, idlers and cutpurses milled about the great cathedral, whose nave was a place of business, alms-giving and assignations as well as of prayer.

This time Morgan's pace was unusually quick and, with hopes rising, Thomas wondered whether the man had at last ceased his begging for the day. To his relief, instead of entering St Paul's, where Thomas might be detected if he followed, Morgan skirted the south door and took off across Knightrider Street, down the road known as Paul's Chain which led to the river. At least, Thomas told himself, he was much closer to home now. Then, aware of his tiredness, he thought ruefully how hopeless was his plight: he must follow the laughing man to the end, even if he should cross over to Bankside where there was little law and less order.

It was then, in the gloomy evening, with lights springing up all about the city, that he

almost lost Morgan for the last time. The beggar had crossed Thames Street and entered Paul's Wharf. Seemingly unaware that he was observed, he ducked suddenly into an alley between unlit, noisome dwellings, and Thomas was hard-pressed to follow. As he turned in behind Morgan he stopped dead, and backed away around the corner, praying that he had not been seen. Morgan was standing in the deserted alley, looking to left and right. But when Thomas dared risk another peep around the corner, the man was gone.

To lose his quarry now, after a whole day of tracking him, seemed more than he could bear. He clenched a fist and would have slammed it against the timbers of the tumbledown building against which he cowered, like a criminal himself, when there was a sound of someone splashing through puddles towards him. Thomas stepped backwards and was about to flatten himself against a wall, when a man in a dark, ragged cloak with a bundle on his back emerged from the alley and stopped dead, facing him. For a moment, both men stared at each other; then the other one broke into a familiar cackle. It was Morgan, of course, minus his hallmark yellow coat and his shambling gait. His work was done for the day; he had stepped out of his role.

Thomas felt like a man in a play who has been thrust on stage without knowing his speech, or even the plot. His feet numb from the cold, his body stiff and tired, he struggled to think of some course of action. But very quickly, the decision was taken out of his hands. Morgan stopped laughing, put two dirty fingers to his mouth and gave a deafening whistle. Then he turned and ran the short distance down Paul's Wharf to the waterfront stairs.

Involuntarily, Thomas followed, and halted at the riverfront, the hackles rising on his neck. There was a wherry below the stairs, with two men in it. More importantly, there came the sound of a footfall from behind him. At that moment, Morgan turned about and faced Thomas, grinning insolently. As Thomas whirled round, something thudded down on his head with the weight of a fence-post, and the wet ground tilted up towards him.

When he awoke, he was lying on a narrow bed in a small room with daylight coming in through a grimy window. The light stabbed at his eyes so that he closed them at once, nausea rising along with a fearful pain in his head. He waited, breathing deeply, until his stomach settled and he dared open his eyes again. When he did, he saw that his boots and jerkin had been removed. He looked about the room. The door, which had a large keyhole in it, was

closed; beside it was a crimson gown of taffeta hanging on a peg. On a rickety table under the window was a candle, a jug and cups, a hand mirror and a collection of cracked pots and jars.

He frowned, aware now of noises from several directions: from below him, and through the

wall beside him, came voices and even laughter, while from the floor above came a dull thudding that increased both in volume and in tempo, until he realized with a start what it was.

'My Lord,' he muttered. 'I'm in a trugging-house.'

He sat up, and the bile rose in his throat, but swallowing it down he struggled to his feet and staggered to the table. He looked into the jug and was relieved to see it nearly full, but when he raised it to his lips he found it contained not water, but wine; cheap hippocras, by the taste. He allowed himself a swallow, then washed his mouth out with more of it, and spat it out on to the floor. At that moment he heard a key grate in the lock and turned to see a very young woman standing in the doorway in a dress cut so low that her breasts were busked out above it. She took one quick look then darted forward, shouting: 'That's my wine, you whoreson sot! I'll make you lick it up!'

He felt dizzy. He leaned on the table, breathing deeply. To his alarm the table-legs immediately gave way and he crashed to the floor in a heap of broken pots and splintered wood. There was a moment's silence, as he put out an arm and raised himself, to see the spindly little trull staring down at him, speechless with indignation.

'Accident,' he croaked, and started to get to his feet, but now came loud footsteps on the stairs outside. His head still spinning, he rested on one knee as a heavy-set man came striding into the room. He looked at Thomas, then pulled a poniard from his belt and, bending close to him, pressed it to his neck.

'Back on the bed.'

Without a word Thomas rose stiffly, crossed to the bed and sat upon it. Still facing him, the man spoke roughly over his shoulder to the girl. 'He was supposed to be tied with cords, you silly little ramp. What's been afoot here?'

But the girl was not in the least intimidated. Placing her hands on her hips she retorted: 'Speak to me like that again, you filthy cuttle, I'll have you up before the sergeant of the Clink. He's a client, don't you know nothing?'

The man swore and turning to her snapped: 'He gets free, you'll need more than a dozen sergeants, you pox-ridden puzzel.'

To Thomas, he said: "Don't try and go downstairs. There's a Cerberus guards the door, would break your arms for sport.'

As the man turned to go Thomas said, as calmly as he could: 'I want to talk to John Lynch.'

The man laughed, an unpleasant laugh without mirth.

Brushing past the girl, he said: 'Nobody of that name here. Ask this little trull.'

Then he went out, slamming the door behind him.

The girl stood looking at him for a moment, then to his surprise she ignored him completely and began picking up her possessions from the floor, all the while muttering to herself.

'Think I've got naught better to do than tidy - with the pocket justice due? Rivelled old rogue'll want me riggish and tricked up like the queen of the night... damn them all for a pot of piss!'

Clearing his dry throat, Thomas asked: 'Will you tell me where I am?'

She turned, picking up shards of broken earthenware, as if only now remembering that he was there. There was a brightness in her eyes that he could not fathom. With a toss of her head, she answered: 'In Heaven.' Her eyes narrowed to a slit. 'And don't think you're getting laced mutton for free, because you're not. They'll souse you later. I've got train-work to do. I'm no fourpenny fillock, me. I'm pure silver!'

Though the words were unfamiliar to him, the meaning was clear enough. In a gentler tone, he said: 'Let me help you clear up.'

At that she rounded on him. 'Don't try and cog me, you runagate scab! You stay there and give thanks they didn't drop you in the river instead of mewing you up here!'

Suddenly, he was aware of a barking of dogs, deep and menacing, from beyond the window. It sounded like a large pack.

'Whose dog's are they?' he asked.

She regarded him as if he were simple-minded. 'It's the kennels. The Bull Ring's back there, don't you even know that?'

At least, he thought, she would talk to him. He sought to get information while he might.

'Who brought me here? John Lynch's men?'

She said nothing, merely rose to her feet and threw the broken pots into a corner. Then she gave a cry and scooped to pick up the little hand-mirror, which was cracked across.

'You...!' she scowled at him, almost in tears. She was a child, he saw now, of no more than

thirteen or fourteen years.

'If I get away from here, I'll buy you a bigger looking-glass than that,' he said. 'With a frame of rosewood.'

She stared. 'You're a lying, canting knave.'

He shook his head. 'I swear on my daughter's heart. She is at home, on the Downs in

Berkshire. We're country people.'

He strove to befriend her, to make her see him not as an enemy but as a man. When she said nothing, he pressed on.

'I was following someone I thought would bring me to Lynch. Some of his men did a terrible deed - killed four falcons, broke their necks. I'm a falconer - you understand? I want justice.'

She was looking oddly at him. 'Killed four falcons?'

He nodded. At once the brightness came back into her eyes, and she gave a shriek of laughter. 'You're a simpler, and that's all such folk as you are fit for. I could foist your pocket myself!'

She went off into another fit of laughter, and his heart sank. She was a poor, slow-witted creature; some unwanted child sold to the trugging-house, raised to the work of the sisterhood, knowing little else but crime and debauchery. She was a perfect keeper, because she cared not who he was, or why he was here.

He lay back on the bed and tried to rest as she turned away, humming to herself, and gazed into the broken mirror. After a while, he managed to fall asleep, until in the afternoon he was woken by a fearful barking, bellowing and roaring, accompanied by raucous shouts and cheers: The Bull Ring was doing good business.

In the evening, three men came for him.

One was the rogue with the Spanish leather jerkin, who had attacked him in the alley at Pudding Lane. The other, he guessed, was the second assailant, a shorter fellow with thick brows and greasy black hair, who glared at him as if he were eager for any excuse to level the score. The third one, who came in behind the other two, was of a different stamp: a muscular fellow in worn galley-slop breeches with a sword at his belt. One ex-soldier may often recognize another. This was the lieutenant, Thomas saw; the other two were but foot-soldiers.

And not only that; his mouth tightened when he saw that the newcomer had fresh scars on his left cheek, and a torn ear lobe. Here before him, was the slaughterer of the falcons.

As Thomas sat up on the bed, the first ruffian threw his boots down and told him to put them on. He did so, while they stood in a semi-circle and watched his every move. There would be no chance with these men. As he straightened up, one of them slammed a fist into his stomach.

'That's by way of instruction,' the scarred man said. 'Come with us and say naught, and mayhap you'll not get another.'

Gasping, he drew himself erect, whereupon they parted and made way for him. The girl was nowhere to be seen. Unsteadily he walked out to the passage, and down a creaking staircase. From various rooms in the house, the sounds of pleasure reached him. The three men walked close behind, as he descended slowly to the ground floor. Ahead a door was open, and beyond it a spiked gate giving on to the street. As he walked outside, a huge figure in a sleeveless jerkin and a scarlet cap loomed over him. Looking up, he saw the dark face of the gatekeeper, or 'Cerberus', that most houses of sin employed to deal with every difficulty, from dissatisfied customers to the hapless enforcers of the law. The man was an African, big and strong as a bear, with arms that could have crushed Thomas like a chicken. With a chuckle, he moved aside and watched him, surrounded by his bodyguard, step into the street. Then, with a man at either arm, the prisoner was marched briskly away.

The street bordered the river, and at last he realized that he was on its south shore. After knocking him senseless at Paul's Wharf, they had bundled him into the boat and crossed over to Bankside. And almost every house they passed was a brothel.

The place was lively. Men - always men - passed to and fro. They were of every station, from fashionable townsmen in wasp-waisted doublets and round hose, to artisans and serving-men in threadbare linen. Most ignored Thomas; some looked at him with frank curiosity. Nobody spoke to him, even when they passed a rowdy alehouse with a sagging jutty that almost brushed the top of his head. The drinkers, some standing in the doorway with pipes and tankards, merely eyed him as he passed. Then the party rounded a corner and stopped abruptly outside a narrow-fronted house, all the windows of which were boarded or shuttered. One man rapped on the door, which was flung open immediately, and Thomas was pushed inside. Blinking in the dim light, he saw a figure seated at a table. The man raised a crooked finger and beckoned him forward.

As he approached, Thomas heard the door close behind him. Before him sat a rather small man of middle years, with short- cropped hair and a cropped beard, and the cruellest face he

had ever seen.

'Hear you've been looking for me, master tall falconer,' he said, and a grin that was more of a sneer spread across his face, revealing a few blackened teeth. 'I'm John Lynch.'

From behind Thomas now came a screeching laugh that stopped his blood. Here too was Laughing Morgan, ambling forward with his arms outstretched and swaying from side to side, as if to remind him of a part he had played; or mayhap of an old joke the two of them had once shared.

And so it was, apparently: a kind of joke, to Lynch and his associates, all of whom joined Morgan in prolonged, uproarious and cruel laughter. Thomas stood like a tethered beast, as they closed about him. He had found his quarry; or more accurately, it was they who had found him.

CHAPTER 12

For some moments after the laughter died away, nothing was said. Lynch seemed genuinely curious about the man who stood before him. His eyes, never still, moved about Thomas's face and body, missing no detail. Finally, he made a gesture, and someone shoved a chair across the floor with his boot.

'You don't look in the best of health, falconer,' Lynch said, with a snort. 'Best sit down. Find us some brandy, Master Cook.'

Thomas sat heavily as the scarred man brought a bottle and cups and set them down on the table between Lynch and his prisoner.

Lynch poured a generous measure into each and raised one to his lips. Thomas remained still and silent, until Lynch put down his cup and said: 'Bravado is a poor cloak for a condemned man, falconer. You've neither eaten nor drunk today. Take while you can; that philosophy has seldom failed me.'

Now that he was at last face to face with the man, Thomas began to feel an odd sort of relief, and a stirring of his courage. It was fuelled by a burning anger. Here about him were the men who had been responsible for all his ills: the senseless slaughter of the magnificent birds, the beating he had taken back in the city, the frightening of Lady Margaret...

On a sudden impulse to find out everything whatever the consequences, he asked:

'Which of you killed Nathaniel Pickering?'

The silence that fell was so intense, he was suddenly aware that he could hear the lapping of the river, beyond the wall to his right. The tide was rising. From further off, his keen hearing picked out the cries of the watermen. Only yards away, the bustle and business of London carried on as normal.

Lynch spoke coldly. 'That name means naught to me, and you're a bold javel to be asking questions. But I'll ask you some, and you'll speak the truth or I'll have Master Cook put the rope round your pate.'

His eyes strayed to the scarred man, who had sat down on a heavy oak chest against the wall. In his hands was a short length of thick cord, its ends looped around a narrow billet of wood.

'Master Cook has worked for many an inquisitor,' Lynch expanded, with a faint grin. 'He's not particular so long as he's paid.'

Thomas fought to ignore the fear which was spreading through his vitals. It was a simple technique: the tightening of a rope around the victim's head. And like most direct methods, it seldom failed to work. Sooner or later he would break down. In the condition he was in it would likely be sooner.

The other men, Laughing Morgan included, had seated themselves about the room, helping themselves to drink. Now that his eyes had adjusted to the poor light, Thomas saw that it had once been an alehouse. There was even a row of old barrels against one wall. The damp flagstones were worn smooth from years of heavy use. At the rear was a door, heavily bolted. There were packages of various sizes piled beside it. This place filled many functions, but paramount among them no doubt, was that of a receiving-house for stolen property.

'First, I have sorrowful news to impart to you,' Lynch said, in a sympathetic tone. 'Your friend, the old soldier from the Black Bull, passed away yesterday.'

Thomas returned the man's gaze, trying not to react, but with the hopeless feeling that there would be no escape for him, either. As if reading his thoughts, Lynch gave a nod.

'Drowned in the river, poor woodcock. A man must have care where he puts his foot, in these times. Even the Queen of Scots is finding that out.'

There was a snigger from the others. Lynch took another drink. Thomas stared defiantly, though his stomach churned as he added Selden's murder to the list of this man's atrocities.

'Now,' Lynch said, wiping his mouth with the sleeve of his jerkin, 'tell me why you followed my friend Morgan here.'

Thomas hesitated. A plan had sprung unbidden into his mind. It was not much, but he had few choices before him.

'To find you,' he said.

'Why?' Lynch asked. 'There's no matter between us that I know of.'

'The breaking of those falcons' necks may be as nothing to you,' Thomas said. 'To me it is a coward's cruelty, worse than any deed I can compass.'

Cook stirred and let out a long breath that fell short of a growl, but stayed where he was. Lynch was watching Thomas.

'I did hear you're a friend to beasts,' he said softly. Thomas felt his brow crease involuntarily. Someone had said that to him, not very long since; who it was, he could not remember.

Suddenly Lynch yawned. 'You're a fool who wouldn't heed fair warning. And yet, you're naught but a servant, when all's done,' he added. 'A louse, to be shaken off and crushed.'

'You've pried long enough.'

He looked away, as if bored with the game. One of the other ruffians, Thomas could not see which, fidgeted and gave a cough. He sensed now that this interview was but a short prelude to a quick exit. He forced himself to try the offensive.

'There are other matters, that do touch on a quarrel of yours,' he said. Lynch's eyes slid across to his; he waited.

'You know I speak of a lady.'

Lynch's mouth tightened. Quickly Thomas added: 'Not my mistress. The younger one.'

Lynch clenched a fist and made an odd circling motion with it about the table, as if controlling the urge to smash it down. Surprised at the ease with which he had provoked him, Thomas spoke further. 'I have more knowledge of this than you think. Mayhap we should speak of it alone.'

But now, Lynch's face showed a suppressed rage so vile and so deep, that if vented it might consume the entire room and everyone in it. Thomas saw, in that moment, how dangerous the man was. This was how he kept such an unruly rabble at his beck and call. Even Cook, sitting with arms folded tight about him, showed a trace of unease.

When Lynch spoke, it was in a controlled manner, but the threat was there now in his eyes, and would not depart until sated.

'You'll be alone soon enough, you marbled javel, your neck adorned with twined hemp. I'll have them cut you down before death, as they do with traitors, and draw your bowels out. I can have one shin up the bridge after dark and stick your head on a pole with the others. The kites will peck your skull clean.'

Thomas eyed him steadily. There was a way here, he told himself, if he might delve for it.

'Then you'll not learn what I know.'

'I'll learn it, and more!' Lynch snapped out. 'When my fellows are done with you you'll spill all you have, and beg to be allowed to spill more!'

'But would you want them to hear all of it?' Thomas said, dropping his voice as if in confidence. There was another tense silence, like the one that fell when he had mentioned the death of Nathaniel. This time Cook spoke up.

'Let me squeeze him,' he said in a flat, dry voice. 'Send the others out, if you desire it. I'll stop my ears with cloths, then I'll not hear what he says.'

Lynch gave a smile and nodded. But quickly, Thomas answered: 'I'll spill it before they get out the door.'

They were at the gaming-table: the dice were Lynch's and no doubt cogged in his favour, but still Thomas had a hope that he could win. He risked a knowing smile, as if to show that

his confidence had some real basis.

Lynch half-raised himself from his chair and smashed his stoneware cup against the side of Thomas's head.

For a moment Thomas felt nothing except the sting of the brandy in his eyes, then sharp pain shot across his cheek below his ear and he felt blood ooze forth. He blinked, shook himself and put a hand to his face, which seemed to break the tension. There was rapid movement from all sides, his arms were pulled roughly behind his back and he was pinioned. Now, Cook stood up and began placing the rope about his head. From somewhere in the rear came Morgan's cackling laugh.

Lynch stood and faced him across the table. 'I will gag you so that you may not speak,' he said, 'and then my tame wolf can proceed. Will that not pink your false pride, you ruffling dog?'

Thomas felt the blood running down his face and on to his collar. He took a deep breath and, without fully understanding why he did it, said: 'I know how you may win her favour. You have failed thus far, because you have used the pike. The poniard's the weapon you want.'

But glowering with rage, Lynch shouted: 'You'll not instruct me!'

Thomas's breath came now in short bursts, as the coarse rope tightened across his brow. From the corner of his eye he saw Cook twist the stick, then stop. With the next turn, the pain would come. Lynch meanwhile, had taken a soiled kerchief from his pocket and was fashioning it into a gag. They would have their way with him now and his ploy had done nothing but provoke them. Trying to keep the panic out of his voice, he hissed:

'She wishes to see you again and set a stratagem before you. With what I know, you may come at her riches!'

Lynch leaned close to Thomas, so that he could smell the stench upon his breath.

'You're lying to me. You have naught to trade.'

'She's your daughter Susanna!' Thomas threw back. 'And I have learned her secret!'

He closed his eyes then, not wishing to see the rope twist, for he was certain that he would now pay dearly for his tactics. He had shot his last bolt; the fact that he knew of Lynch's spoiled courtesan daughter would avail him nothing.

But nothing happened.

He opened his eyes and Lynch was there still, his face barely eighteen inches away. Wheels grated within the man's dark mind, so that one might almost watch them. His henchmen stirred impatiently on either side of Thomas; he smelt their sweat and the rank odour of their unwashed clothes. But at last, the petty tyrant raised a hand. With a gasp,

Thomas found his arms free. The men stepped back, and Cook, though unwillingly, slackened the rope and lifted it from his head.

Lynch sank slowly down into his chair. After a moment, he told the other men to go outside.

They did not like the order, but stood and shuffled about on the stone floor. Cook said: 'He's cogging you - he's got nothing to trade with. Let me prove it.'

He held up the rope. He looked now like a man who had looked forward to a banquet and been thrown scraps instead. But Lynch shook his head impatiently and said: 'I'll hear what he claims he has. Then you can do as you please.'

They turned about and went to the door then, even Laughing Morgan, who wheezed a little. Cook, the last to go, leaned close to Thomas's ear as he passed, and said: 'I'll crack your skull like a duck-egg, you whoreson knave.'

It was then that Thomas remembered the earring. He reached into his pocket, drew it forth and threw it on to the table, where it landed with a tinkle. Cook and Lynch stared.

'I took it off the falcon that spoiled your face,' Thomas said. 'You're lucky you still have your eyes.'

Cook breathed deeply and his hand rose, but Lynch forestalled him with a grunt and a jerk of his thumb. The killer straightened up slowly, then followed the others outside, the way they had come in. Thomas was left alone with Lynch.

He had worked out what he would do.

Speed and surprise would be his only allies. Lynch glanced over Thomas's shoulder as the door banged shut behind him, giving him the chance he needed. Without a second's hesitation he raised his hands over his head and brought both fists down with all his strength on top of Lynch's head.

Lynch's face banged down on to the table-top, as his arms came flapping up at his sides like wings. Before he could even open his mouth, Thomas had picked up the earthenware jug and smashed it over his forehead. The man's eyes bulged, and his breath exploded from him like a punctured water-skin, but Thomas did not stay to observe. He simply ran to the far door and unbolted it even as he heard Lynch yell and the street door opening behind him. Flinging the door wide, he stepped out into a passage lined with sacks. There was another door at the end, but as he reached it, it opened outwards, and there stood Laughing Morgan barring the way,

with a billhook in his hand and an evil grin on his face. A moment's hesitation and Thomas knew he would die here. He banged a fist into Morgan's face, thrust him aside, and ran.

He ran through the gathering dusk, across a yard strewn with rubbish, past a foul-smelling soil-heap, crashed through a rotted wicker fence, then ran to the right between two houses and found himself on the Bankside again. Dogs barked in the distance. Across the river, London was a panorama of lights; ahead of him was the sloping shingle beach that led down to the water's edge. Shouts came from behind. Without checking his stride, Thomas ran across the street at full tilt, over the slippery gravel, and leapt into the Thames.

He came up, choking for breath, his movements sluggish in the icy water. As it cleared from his ears he heard more shouting, and something hit the surface inches from his head. Filling his lungs, he dived, and whirling about like an eel underwater, tugged at his heavy boots. Clumsily he got them off, then struck out at an angle, breaking the surface again some yards further off, his lungs bursting. Turning his head, he risked a look backwards and saw a group on the shore, shouting and pointing. But there were no boats near them, he saw with relief, and striking out further, he began a steady crawl against the current. He was swimming for his life, and weak though he was, he would fight to the last gasp. Mercifully, the tide was incoming, otherwise he would have been swept downstream towards the bridge. He kicked his legs out, and headed further into mid-stream, where he now grew aware of other voices, ahead of him and to his right. A wave washed over his head, filling his mouth. When he raised his face above the water, coughing and choking, he saw a boat sculling towards him. He tried to shout, but only a grunt came out. He was aware of a light-headedness; his arms, numb from the cold and the effort, did not seem to be working properly. As the boat bore down upon him he saw a bearded face staring down at him over the gunwale. He began to go under, then got his head clear again, struggling to tread water, as the man shouted to him. An oar appeared, inches from his face. Thomas grasped it with both hands, then held on like a leech as a pair of strong arms drew him towards the boat, which wobbled dangerously. Then he banged his head against the side, and everything went dark.

He must have blacked out only for seconds, for as his senses returned, Thomas found he

was hanging half over the side, and the waterman was struggling to pull him aboard without capsizing his boat. Reaching out to grasp the seat, he pulled himself forward and landed in a heap in the bottom, fighting for breath. As he lay there like a drowned sheep, he heard a thud against the side of the boat. The waterman had leaped to his station and was heaving at the oars with all his strength, shouting something.

Thomas could not make out what he said, until

another thud came just above his head. To his horror, the timbers splintered and a sharp point appeared, stuck fast in the gunwale.

'One of the bastards got a crossbow!' The boatman was yelling. 'They're shooting at us!'

Ducking his head low, he rowed his little vessel hard across the wide, slow-moving Thames towards the London shore. No more shots came. Thomas could only lie exhaustedly in the bottom of the boat and let himself be carried away.

CHAPTER 13

That night, after lights had been snuffed out in the many windows of Sir Marcus Brooke's house on the river, Jane Bull was bolting and locking the rear doors before checking that the maids were all abed. Since Saturday night, when Lady Margaret's bold young servant had managed to unlock the yard door and sneak out to the stables, she had been told by Sir Marcus to be more vigilant, even though Lady Margaret and her party were now gone. Sir Robert Vicary had arrived that morning in a poor temper and taken his wife away at once, along with Catherine and James the groom. This last fact was the subject of much gossip and speculation in the servants' hall. Of even greater interest however, and of more concern to Jane, was the fact that they had left without Thomas the falconer.

The housekeeper crossed the yard from the wash-house to the kitchen, the keys on their ring jangling at her waist. Her thoughts had been in turmoil since yesterday, when Thomas had gone off somewhere and not returned. The talk was that Sir Robert had dismissed him from his service, and that if and when he eventually reappeared, he and his poor young daughter would be cast out of their cottage.

The night was clear and chilly, with a half-moon. As Jane reached the door, there came a sound from some yards away. She whirled about, her thoughts leaping at once to the intruder at the window, though that was almost a week ago. Then to her surprise, somebody called her name.

It was low, little more than a hoarse whisper, but she knew the voice. With a glance towards the house, she hurried across the garden to where two box-hedges met at right angles to form an arched bower. There she halted, and her hand went to her mouth.

Thomas was slumped on the seat like a drunken man, arms at his sides. His clothes were muddy. His hair hung damp about his face, which bore the marks of every kind of hurt: a gash caked with blood on his left cheek, a lump on the forehead, dirt and bruises and an overall weariness that seemed to pull him down into sleep, even as he spoke.

'I fear to involve you,' he whispered. 'But there's no other.'

With a sigh, she sat down beside him, and reached out a hand. As she touched his face, he said in a voice of utter weariness: 'Can you get me into the stables? I must rest.'

She frowned anxiously. Her urge to help him was tempered by the sudden realization that, despite the intimacy they had shared, she barely knew him. What terrible things might he have done?

Somehow, he guessed her thoughts. 'I've harmed no one,' he said. 'I've broken no law that I

know of. Yet I must not be discovered - there's much to do, and no one to help.'

Instinctively, she made up her mind to believe him. The resolve spurred her to action. 'In the stable, you would soon be discovered - as you would in any of the outhouses,' she said. 'Sir Marcus has them searched every morning and night.'

A look of helplessness passed across his face, but quickly she added: 'I'll take you to my room. No one will look there.'

He shook his head slowly, but she would not be gainsaid. Standing, she asked: 'Can you walk to the house?'

He did not answer, but struggled to his feet, grunting with pain, though she could not yet see the cause. As she put out a hand to steady him, she exclaimed: 'Merciful heaven, your clothes are wringing wet.'

He grimaced. 'The river saved my life.'

With her help he walked slowly and stiffly up the garden and in through the kitchen door, which she closed and swiftly bolted. The warmth of the room, with its pleasant smell of new-baked bread from the ovens, made him giddy. He sank to a bench by the long table, but Jane's voice whispered urgently: 'Don't! You fall asleep now I'll never wake you, nor can I carry you.'

Painfully he raised himself, leaning his weight on her shoulder and like two soldiers come from the fight they shuffled towards the back stairs. How he climbed them he did not remember later, except that she told him she pushed him from behind, all the while terrified someone would hear. When finally he staggered into the small, familiar room and fell on to the bed, she noticed for the first time that he had no boots, only torn and filthy stockings, which were stained with blood. How far he had walked in that condition, she dared not imagine, she merely lifted his legs and placed them on the bed, where he lay like a dead man and fell asleep at once.

He knew nothing of how she went down in her bare feet to fetch a basin of water and cloths; how she stripped him and washed his body from head to toe, and put a dressing on his face; nor of how when she saw the cuts and abrasions on his feet, with the gravel embedded so deeply in places she had to pick it out with a needle, she commenced to weeping. He knew nothing of it, but slept the impenetrable sleep of one who has survived a battle, yet almost spent himself in the process.

In the morning when he woke and memories of where he was and all that had happened

welled up, he was at a loss what to do. He lay peacefully in Jane's bed and listened to the

sounds of the household going about its business. Outside it was another bright October day, and he should be far away, on the Downs with his hawks. Then he thought of Lady Margaret, and of Eleanor, and a heavy weight settled over him.

This would never do. By the time Jane Bull came in later, wearing a cap and apron and an anxious look, he had decided on a course.

'You must tell Sir Marcus,' he said.

She sat down on the bed and put out a hand, and he took it and squeezed it gently. 'I can but thank you for what you did. I will not draw you into my troubles. You have your position here.'

She nodded saying: 'They already suspect something. I could never hide anything from Lady Alice for long.'

'I'll arise at once,' he said. 'Tell Sir Marcus I'll wait on him and explain myself.'

She told him then about Sir Robert and Lady Margaret's departure, and how since it appeared he had abandoned his mistress and gone off to London for some purpose of his own, Sir Robert was turned against him. He listened in silence, then said: 'All I've done has gone awry. I've blundered about like a fool... I've not used my head.'

She looked directly at him. 'Mayhap you soared too high seeking sweeter airs, when pleasant enough ones already lay before you.'

His eyes dropped. 'Then I was a fool twice over.'

She rose, and going to the door, said: 'I'll see if I can borrow some clothes for you. Yours are washed and drying on the bushes, though they'll need more patches than a beggar's cloak.' Then she left him lying in her bed with a heavy heart. The future was a dark forest before him. Yet there were surprises in store for him, when an hour later, having eaten a little food and dressed himself in clean clothes, he stood before Sir Marcus Brooke like a penitent. On his feet were borrowed boots, a little small but serviceable. The deep cut on his cheek, made by the cup that Lynch had wielded, was raw and swollen.

Sir Marcus was not alone in the hall. Thomas had expected the fearsome Lady Alice to be present, but instead there stood a tall man in a lawyer's gown and high ruff, with beard trimmed neatly to a steeple's point. The man stared at him curiously.

'Well, falconer,' Sir Marcus began drily. 'I'll gamble you've a pretty tale to tell us.'

He stood and told it, as clearly as he could, beginning with the killing of the gyrfalcons, of

which Sir Marcus already knew. Carefully he omitted all reference to Lady Margaret; he tried rather to draw a picture of his own attempts to discover the perpetrators of the crime. Nor did he think it necessary to speak of Matthew Selden. When he finished with an account of his escape from Lynch by water, and of making his way home on foot, there was a short silence.

It was not Sir Marcus, but the other man who spoke. 'You have left nothing out?' he asked, gazing shrewdly at Thomas.

Stiffly, Thomas answered that he had not.

'Well,' the man replied, 'for a falconer, and a stranger to London, you seem quite an accomplished intelligencer.'

Thomas said nothing.

'This gentleman is Doctor Perkins,' Sir Marcus explained. 'He is a lawyer.'

Thomas inclined his head politely. Perkins asked him: 'What do you know of a man named Nicholas Stocker?'

'He was lawyer to my ladyship's late brother, Master Nathaniel,' Thomas answered. 'More than that, I cannot say.'

Perkins glanced at Sir Marcus. Thomas had an uneasy feeling that they knew more of Lady Margaret's affairs than he realized.

'I'm a hawking man, as you know,' Sir Marcus said, looking not unkindly at Thomas. 'I would trust a man like, let us say Jack Roker, the Earl of Stafford's astringer, with my life; more than that, I would trust him with my goshawk.' He allowed himself a smile. 'And Jack it seems, trusts you. On such short acquaintance as you had, that is a rare phenomenon.'

Thomas waited. Sir Marcus walked a few paces before the great fireplace and said: 'I will lend you a horse. I will also write a letter for you to carry to your master, when you return to Petbury - as you must do presently and give a good account of yourself. Sir Robert values you highly, falconer. He has been much grieved by your behaviour. Yet he will surely understand that this is so foreign to your true nature, it must have had good cause.'

Thomas froze inwardly. They were going to ask him what his deeper motives had been. How could he hope to shield Lady Margaret?

'A warrant will be sworn out against this Lynch,' Sir Marcus went on. 'I will have a company of stout men, well-armed, comb every inch of Bankside until he is found - and his parcel of ruffians too. Their crimes shall bring them to Newgate, and I'll lay odds, thence to Tyburn.'

'Cook, the ex-soldier,' Thomas said, relieved at this turn of conversation. 'I believe he killed Master Nathaniel. He's skilled with a crossbow.'

'Then he will hang for sure,' Perkins put in, gazing evenly at Thomas. 'But...' he paused, a cool smile on his lips. 'I am puzzled, Master Finbow. Why would such a fellow travel seventy miles to the wilds of Berkshire, to lie in wait for a man he has never seen, and shoot him off his horse?'

That jolted him. Still smiling, Perkins asked: 'Does it not appear that Lynch has what the Italians term a *vendetta* of some nature against your mistress and her family?'

'So it would appear, sir,' Thomas answered, and tried to show by his expression that the matter were a puzzle to him, too.

Sir Marcus now addressed him. 'Sir Robert is my close and valued friend, falconer. I would spare no pains to assist him, if I thought there was some threat to his safety - or to his reputation.'

The meaning was not spelled out, but Thomas began to understand. It had been there all along - when Stocker had told Lady Margaret she had no legal powers. This was men's talk; if Lady Margaret had some dark secret, it must be penetrated, then resolved - not for her satisfaction, but for that of her husband. His honour must be protected, at all costs.

'You begin to soar a little, falconer,' Sir Marcus said quietly. 'You are keen-eyed enough to see.'

Thomas tried to order his thoughts. In his heart, he knew he would never betray Lady Margaret. If there were some way to help uncover the things she feared, then deal with them swiftly and discreetly, so that the secret was buried once and for all... Just now it seemed a momentous task, a burden that he longed to cast off. He was alone - but here was help being offered: if he told these men all, he would be restored to Sir Robert's service, and to his favour. He would be free to go back to his old life, and everything he valued. It was easy.

But what then would become of Lady Margaret?

He looked up and saw the two men watching him closely, taking a deep breath, he asked: 'Might I be allowed a few days in which to recover from my hurts, Sir Marcus? Then I will return to my master as you have described and beg his forgiveness. It was not my place to go scouring London for those men without his warrant - or that of my mistress. She knows little of my doings. I believe the matter is as much of a mystery to her, as to you.'

There was tension in the silence that followed, but Thomas pressed forward, keeping emotion out of his voice. 'If you will loan me enough money to be repaid by my master when I reach Petbury, I believe I can find another gyrfalcon and purchase it for him, as I was first sent here to do. That is all I desire.'

He stood stiff as a man-at-arms then, and waited, staring at the wall opposite. From the corner of his eye he saw Perkins frown impatiently. But Sir Marcus seemed unperturbed. Had Thomas not just rejected his invitation to spill everything he knew? Or, was his loyalty merely being tested? As this thought sank home, Sir Marcus spoke, briskly now. 'I will grant what you ask. You may leave here on Thursday, and no later. Remember that you may be recalled to serve as a witness, should it prove necessary.'

Perkins seemed impatient to speak, though not in front of Thomas. His eyes were busy signalling to Sir Marcus. Greatly relieved, Thomas bowed and thanked the knight for his kindness.

Sir Marcus grunted. 'Am I kind? Some might call me a fool, for putting up with so many sorts of impudence under my own roof. I've lost my best groom on account of a servant's maidenhead.'

Thomas wanted to laugh. But at the expression on Sir Marcus's face, he nodded gravely and turned to leave.

'And stay out of Lady Alice's sight,' Sir Marcus added, 'or I'll be tongue-lashed into altering my plans.' With a quick bow at both men, Thomas gained the doorway and was outside the room, where he could let out a deep breath.

He went first to put Jane's mind at rest but was told she had gone to the market. Though still sore and aching from his wounds, he hurried then to turn his thoughts into deeds. He had two days in which to act. He had resolved to explore every thicket of this tangled affair, until he found what he sought. Though he was still unsure precisely what that was, he had found tracks at least; and tracks must lead somewhere. Within the hour, he was walking northwards across the fields by Holborn and Hampstead, and uphill to the village of Highgate. At his belt was a full purse, furnished by Sir Marcus, and also a borrowed dagger. The morning was fresh, with some cloud scudding from the south-west, and it was good to be outdoors. By the end of the week, he would be home, come what may, and would see his Eleanor.

But first, he would find John Pollard; and he would not let him alone until he had gleaned every grain of information from the scholar's lanky frame.

In Highgate village, Thomas made enquiries at several large houses before he found the one at which Master Pollard served as tutor to two young boys, sons of a wealthy merchant. Going to the house, he was told the family were at dinner, whereupon he asked the serving-man who opened the door to convey an important message to Master Pollard: that the falconer from Petbury was here and must speak to him urgently on a matter known to them both. Then he crossed the street to a tavern, went inside and ordered a mug of ale.

As expected, the scholar appeared some minutes later, stooping in the doorway, in his familiar grey clothes. He saw Thomas, came to his table and sat down without looking him in the eye.

'If you've come to demand money of me, I've precious little,' he said in a haughty voice.

'That's not my purpose,' Thomas told him. 'But if you won't answer my questions, truthfully and in full, I'll not scruple to tell your new employer of your feelings towards Master William Vicary.'

Pollard's eyes dropped. With barely a glance at him, Thomas called for ale for them both. The scholar waited until the drawer had brought it and moved off, then said; 'I have but a short time. There are lessons to give.'

'Then I'll be swift,' Thomas said. 'I want to know all that Nathaniel told you, touching Lady Margaret.'

Pollard took a drink, casting his eyes furtively about like a stage conspirator. He was not cut out for trickery, Thomas thought, and almost pitied him when he blurted: 'I was a knave to threaten her as I did - I've never stooped so low. I was in torment... If she had but given me enough money, I would be out of England by now, never to see her again.'

'Your troubles are not my concern,' Thomas said. 'I want an answer to my question.'

Pollard hesitated, then muttered: 'He told me there was a child born out of wedlock. When Lady Margaret was but eighteen years of age.'

'And then?'

'And then?' Pollard echoed. 'Would that not be enough, if her husband was informed, to cause distress—'

'That's not all,' Thomas cut in sharply, under his breath. 'Don't try me, Master Pollard. I'm in the mire myself, and I'll pull you under with me, if I must.'

The scholar's eyes flitted uneasily towards him.

'It was Nathaniel who took away the child, was it not? Thomas asked.

After a moment, Pollard nodded.

'Where was it placed?'

Pollard's brow puckered. 'That I know not. Killed, or sold in secret like a whore's brat - what does it matter?'

Thomas stared hard at him, so that he fidgeted and added: 'The child is not the nub of it, falconer. It's the identity of the father.'

Thomas took a pull from his ale, apparently unconcerned, but his pulse was racing. Putting

the mug down, he said: 'Nathaniel knew who the father was.'

'Of course,' Pollard snorted. 'Else what power had he over his sister, to keep her on tenterhooks as he did?'

'The father was a nobleman,' Thomas guessed aloud, then wished he had not. A faint gleam came into Pollard's slate-blue eyes.

'You are cold, falconer. Cold as Christmas.'

'Then set me right.'

But Pollard drained his mug and said: 'I was not told all.'

Thomas put out a hand and grasped Pollard by the collar of his thin doublet. 'I've already come close to losing my life, not to mention my livelihood, Master Pollard,' he said. 'Tell me who the father of her child was, or I'll march you over to that house and tell your mistress about your taste for boys like her sons—'

'Enough!' Pollard said through his teeth. 'I've told you what I know.'

'Not all of it,' Thomas answered, still holding the collar.

'I swear to you,' Pollard said irritably, 'he did not tell me who the father was! A guess, is all I have.'

'Then tell it me.'

Pollard gave the bleakest of smiles. 'I believe he may have been a Spanish priest.'

Thomas let go of the man's collar and let his hand fall in pure astonishment. If that were the case, it might indeed begin to explain a great deal.

'It is clouded in secrets,' Pollard said. 'The old man - Francis Pickering - died sad and broken with the burden his daughter brought upon them. He feared even to go out, or to answer his door, never knowing when a summons might come.'

His face was suddenly bitter. 'I know precisely how that feels, falconer.'

Turning his head, he added with some defiance: 'As soon as I have funds saved, I shall take

ship and leave this pestilent country, for the English college at Reims. My hopes rested on Queen Mary - *my* queen - to restore the true religion to this fetid pool of sin.' His gorge rose; it was all he could do to keep his voice below the tavern murmur.

'Now she is on trial for her life, and we are undone by a wicked plot hatched by our enemies!'

Two men at a nearby table looked askance at him, but Pollard no longer cared. He banged a fist down on the board and cried out: 'There is no peace for such as me!'

He got clumsily to his feet and looking down at Thomas, said harshly: 'Now inform on me

and be damned, falconer. You're naught but a savage like all the rest!'

And turning about he blundered to the entrance and went outside, barely remembering to stoop so that the top of his head almost struck the lintel. The door banged loudly behind him.

CHAPTER 14

As afternoon wore on, Thomas walked the lanes back towards London and entered the city by Aldersgate. Passing the Black Bull Inn, he had a sudden impulse to go inside and announce the death of Matthew Selden, adding his intention to see the intruders found and hanged. He knew of course that it would avail him nothing, except perhaps abuse. His thoughts were in turmoil; it seemed he had a different trail to follow. While he tried to think in which direction to turn, he reasoned, he should at least make good one promise - to buy a gyrfalcon.

Tortuously, he made his way through the crowded city by West Cheap and Poultry, recalling his long, damp ordeal of last Sunday when he had followed Laughing Morgan. This Tuesday the beggars were in force at their usual stations, but there was no sign of a yellow coat.

From Lombard Street to Little Eastcheap and thence by Botolph Lane to Thames Street took but a half-hour of walking, until he fetched up again on the crowded Keys and stopped outside the shop of Henry van Velsen. Today the doors were wide, there were customers among the squawking birds in their cages and the Dutchman was in better spirits than when Thomas had seen him last. His face grew sober, however, when he saw the falconer; perhaps he expected to have to repay the considerable sum that Lady Margaret had given him. When Thomas told him that the men who broke into his shop had been discovered, the phlegmatic dealer was almost excited.

'I won't wait for the sheriff's men,' he said. 'I talk with the elders of our church. We spread word among the Nederlanders - go to Bankside, find 'em! You - you come with us, show the way!'

Thomas stood dumbfounded at the news that he was now expected to join a mob. He was about to make some reply when the Dutchman, peering closer at him, said: 'You been hurt. They do this to you, those bad men?'

Thomas nodded, whereupon van Velsen took him by the arm and pulled him towards the rear of the shop.

'Come, sit, my friend,' the Dutchman said. 'I bring wine.' Thomas followed him, somewhat embarrassed, then stopped in his tracks. In one of the big cages at the rear of the shop, a pair of gryfalcons perched, blinking at him through the wickerwork.

'Fine hawks, yes?' Van Velsen smiled at him. 'They's komm from Holland. Your mistress paid - you take?'

Thomas looked the birds over: a female, bright-eyed and strong, and a tercel. With a swelling of his heart he turned to the Dutchman. 'I will. I'll return tomorrow or the day after. Can you get me a carrying-cage, to strap on a horse?'

Van Velsen nodded. 'And repay remainder of money. Van Velsen always pays.'

Greatly relieved, Thomas accepted the offer of a glass of wine and a seed cake. The Dutchman sat with him, eager for details of the killers of the falcons. Thomas managed to talk him out of marching to Bankside: the authorities would act. Finally, van Velsen nodded reluctantly, adding grimly that he would demand redress, one way or another.

By the time Thomas took his leave, he had decided to pay one more call. He asked for directions to Sything Lane. In fact, van Velsen told him, it was close by; if he followed Thames Street for a hundred yards towards the Tower then turned left into Bear Lane, the street he sought was directly opposite.

The afternoon was drawing late, and he had no time to waste. If he had become any kind of intelligencer, as Perkins had described him, then he would begin by finding out all he could about what occurred in Francis Pickering's old house.

A breeze had sprung up, with a scent of autumn discernible even among the smells of the city. At home in Berkshire, the leaves would be falling. Thomas walked the short distance towards the eastern edge of London below Great Tower Hill, turned down Sything Lane and stood once again outside the empty house, the childhood home of Lady Margaret.

It was still empty and just as forlorn, with the gate half off its hinges and the broken window panes. He did not intend to waste time in looking; he had been inside and knew that whatever secrets the old house had once held, answers must now be sought elsewhere.

At that moment the gates of the next house opened, and an elderly gentleman in a hat and richly-trimmed gown emerged. Thomas looked away and made as if to move off, but the old man paid him no heed, turning to his right and walking slowly off up the street. Here was another unexpected piece of luck this day: for peering out of the gate watching the master of the house depart like an anxious mother-hen, was his grey-haired servant, wearing the same frayed cap she had done exactly a week ago.

Without hesitation Thomas strode towards her, gave a short bow and asked: 'Mistress Hall? Eliza Hall?'

The old woman jumped so sharply, her feet almost left the ground. Retreating backwards through the gateway, she snapped; 'Who're you?'

But as he opened his mouth to explain, she remembered. 'You were here last week, with

Margaret Pickering!'

He nodded. 'I would beg a moment of you, mistress,' he said. 'Her ladyship is troubled. Mayhap you can help me discover why?'

'I?' The old woman stared suspiciously. 'I have done naught untowards.'

Thomas smiled and gave a shake of his head. 'It is intelligence I seek, of things past. As much as twenty years past.'

Eliza Hall was silent, but there was a gleam in her eyes: the look of the incorrigible gossip. She looked quickly up and down the street, then said: 'Come to the buttery.'

He followed her to the back of the house and across a yard, and within minutes was sat before a fireplace in Eliza Hall's kitchen. Two young maids were quickly despatched about their duties by the sharp-tongued old woman, who promptly sat down facing Thomas, and said: 'Someone should fetch a priest, to sprinkle holy water over that house.'

Thomas chose his words carefully. 'You believe there has been some evil there, mistress?'

She nodded eagerly. 'He was a wizard, old Master Francis - boiling creatures up in jars and drinking their juices. The Lord knows I was afraid for my life, some nights, of what might come out of that house.'

His attention wavered, as she began a rambling and at times barely coherent account of Lady Margaret's father, the 'wizard'. Much of it was repetition: how the old man kept specimens, unknown creatures brought from overseas; how he drew charts and poured over books at all hours of the night - forbidden books, Eliza would warrant. His son Nathaniel was no better, a wicked man who spent his father's money on every sort of sinful pleasure. It was a strange household, everyone knew; disturbing events occurred there. Especially, Eliza recalled, about the time of the terrible winter, when the river was frozen: that would be in the year of grace, 1565.

'What happened then?' Thomas asked.

She leant closer and whispered: 'That was the year when he got his familiar! As witches do have.'

'What was it like?'

Her eyes gleamed with excitement, so that it was all he could do not to smile. He had a picture of a younger Eliza Hall, twenty years back, peeping at the Pickering house from an upstairs window, hoping to be scared out of her wits.

'I told ye last time: an ape. Like a devil.'

'You saw it, yourself?'

She nodded. 'More than once. Old Francis kept it locked in the house, but it came out at night-time. I saw it in the garden.' She shuddered. 'Black and hairy, like a creature of hell.'

Thomas smiled politely, but his thoughts were busy. At the forefront of them, as it had been for much of the day, was John Pollard's guess that there had at some time been a Spanish priest in the house. If so, his presence would have had to be highly secret. This might sit with Eliza Hall's fanciful account.

'Did it have clothes?' he asked her.

She thought for a moment. 'I believe it did - a cloak wrapped about it, to cover its fearful aspect.'

'Then how do you know it was dark and hairy?'

Her lips tightened. 'Its feet and legs I saw - and it's head! Covered with black hair, and not dressed neat like a man's.'

'Could it not have been a man?' he asked.

She shook her head vehemently. 'It was an ape! Do you doubt my word, master?'

He raised a conciliatory hand. 'I am but eager to discover the truth, mistress.'

'Why not ask your Lady Margaret herself?' she snapped suddenly.

'There are delicate aspects to the matter,' Thomas replied. 'I would not wish to cause distress to her ladyship.'

'She was an odd one herself,' the woman muttered.

Thomas waited, but there came no further comment. Trying a different tack, he asked: 'Was Master Pickering ever rumoured to be a Catholic?'

At that, her manner changed from near-hostility to sudden fear. Drawing back slightly, she asked: 'Are you truly a servant? Or do you hold a different commission?'

He shook his head. 'You saw me, with Lady Margaret. I am but a falconer.'

She frowned. 'What would a falconer want with such news? Hounding papists is not work for such as you.'

He smiled and, inwardly ashamed of employing such flattery, said: 'You are wise, mistress; I should not have attempted to deceive such as you. And I swear that whatever you tell me, shall not go beyond these walls.'

She was excited, as if being asked to take part in unmasking a conspiracy. But summoning

all her dignity, she said: 'It is no secret that old Master Francis was fined for being a recusant.'

So, the old man had not gone to church - the common sign of a Catholic; but there might be other reasons. He delved further.

'Tell me your opinion, mistress: might the strange occurrences you spoke of be explained by the notion that secret masses were being said in that house?'

She was shocked. 'Papist services here - in this street? Where live some of the highest in the land?'

He gave a shrug. Her thoughts tumbling over themselves now, she replied: 'Yes, mayhap it's true - else why would the old man have shunned his neighbours, and hidden himself like a hermit?'

Then, mindful of what she had said, she added: 'Yet, it does not fit. If masses were being said, there would have been people in and out - but visitors were few. At least, as far as I saw.'

Which would be far enough, Thomas thought ruefully.

'The year-old Master Pickering died,' Eliza Hall said with a fearful look, 'was 1580 - the year of the earthquake! God was shaking his rod of anger at all of us, and he struck that old man down soon after, for his wickedness. Is it not plain?'

Thomas said nothing, thinking it was time he took his leave. Then he remembered something she had said on the day they met.

'You spoke of comings and goings at the house.'

'Not then,' she replied, with irritation. 'Of late, I meant - since it was sold.'

'Can you describe them?' She gave a quick shrug. 'Men going inside, taking stuff away. And a lady, in a coach.'

Keeping his face free of expression, he asked what manner of lady that was.

'I did not see,' she answered. 'She never got out of the coach, but waited outside, then drove away. The driver and footman wore a livery.'

'How did you know it was a lady inside?' he asked.

Again, she bristled at his scepticism, and snapped: 'I saw the ends of a gown embroidered with black-work, and a gloved hand with rings upon it. I know there sat a lady!'

'Was the livery known to you?' he asked.

She shook her head. 'My master would know such. He was once a messenger of the Queen's chamber.' She brightened. 'He has but gone to the glasshouse, in Crutched Friars. The Italian

is making him a fine bowl - if you desire, you may wait upon him.'

He smiled and rose, saying: 'I have urgent business myself, mistress. But I do heartily thank you for your conversation.'

Disappointed, she followed him to the door, and asked: 'Do you know what is to become of the empty house?'

Thomas shook his head. At the door, he turned and thanked her again, but she made no reply. As he left the gate, he looked back expecting to see her peering after him, but she was nowhere in sight.

Half an hour later, scarcely taking heed of the route he followed, Thomas passed out of the city by Bishopsgate and found himself before St Botolph's church. Northwards, the suburbs continued past Bedlam hospital and on to Shoreditch, where stood the Old Theatre. The crowds had left now and gone back into the city, but there were many folk still about. This was another of those districts, outside of the authority of the city fathers, with a reputation for pleasures of all kinds, as well as for lawlessness.

On the corner opposite him was an inn called the Dolphin. Facing him, to the right off Bishopsgate Street, a road opened between tightly-packed shops and dwellings, following the curve of the north-east wall round towards Aldgate. He asked a young gallant in a short Spanish cloak and feathered hat who was strutting by, for the name of the street, and was told somewhat disdainfully that it was Houndsditch.

The name brought him up with a jolt. Somewhere along there was the house in which John Lynch's daughter dwelled; the dark lady who had thrown off the shackles of poverty for the fancy ruff and periwig of the courtesan. In the fading light, he gazed at the anonymous row of houses. Knowledge of that woman was Selden's gift to him, for which the honest ex-soldier had paid with his life. He did not intend to see the information wasted. Somehow he knew that this woman was one of the keys to the riddle - perhaps the only key. But how was he to find her, let alone approach her? He did not even know what she looked like, save that she was tall, of rare beauty and dark-complexioned...

He froze, with a frown on his face, and stood staring down at the cobbles. A group of men passed him in garish silk doublets and wide galley-slop breeches, laughing and talking noisily, but he did not see them. He saw Lady Margaret, tall and beautiful; and he saw a Spanish priest, and a notion came to him, so absurd that he almost laughed at it.

Lady Margaret's illegitimate daughter, and the daughter of the villainous John Lynch, were

one and the same.

But no - it could not be possible. He began a fierce debate with himself, while lights appeared in the houses about him. One inner voice told him that he had suspected it already - and it explained so much. Reason this, he told himself: as a wayward girl of eighteen, Margaret Pickering falls in love with a Spaniard, hidden for a time in her father's house because the family are secret Catholics. She bears a child; the priest, perhaps fleeing for his

life, is never seen again. Nathaniel Pickering, cruel and pragmatic, declares the child must be got rid of, not least because of her dark appearance. He makes enquiries of his disreputable friends and is referred to Lynch, an unscrupulous ruffler who'll take the child off his hands and ask no questions. The secret seems safe, and Margaret is later married to Sir Robert Vicary.

But now - suppose Lynch, instead of disposing of the child as he had been told, decides to take her along with him on his travels, and bring her up as his own? She is sweet to look upon, and hence good for business. Soon she is an accomplished kinchin mort, begging at houses for scraps with Lynch's doxy, whom she believes to be her mother. Perhaps she learns to keep householders occupied at the front door while Lynch sneaks in the back and steals. The rest of her life story, or at least the bare thread of it, he had learned from Selden: how she was brutally robbed of her maidenhead; how she ran away to London, and in time made her fortune from her body. What a tale; and yet, was that all it was? The brutal and dangerous world of Lynch and his kind seemed far away from that of the Vicary's and their class... He found himself shaking his head involuntarily. No, another voice told him, it was madness.

He stood up restlessly and began to walk. The matter raised so many questions, he was at a loss. What, if this were true, could he do? Above all, why would Lady Margaret have wanted him to uncover her secret? For she would be ruined if it were revealed, that much was clear.

Then, as he walked through the fields, and the dusk fell, another thought occurred: she did not know! She still believed the child was dead. Indeed, she had believed the entire secret safe until Nathaniel Pickering had come to stay and blackmailed her because of it.

But why then, was Lynch set against Lady Margaret? Was he taking vengeance on her, perhaps hoping to win his daughter's favour, after she had refused to have anything to do with him? Could he have had Nathaniel killed out of vengeance - or to preserve the secret?

Turning the questions over in his mind until he was giddy, Thomas skirted the suburbs of the city by Clerkenwell and Holborn. Finally, he emerged, footsore and exhausted, in the

Strand and made his way to Sir Marcus Brooke's house. He needed to sleep, and then to choose somehow a course of action. He had stumbled upon an answer, though he was far from certain that it was the correct one. And it had many dark and peculiar aspects.

Once again, he walked into Jane Bull's warm kitchen, to looks of surprise and some of suspicion, and sat down without a word. When he fell asleep at the table with his head resting on his arms, nobody disturbed him. He was still there in the early morning, when a scullery maid stumbled in sleepily to rekindle the fire.

CHAPTER 15

In the morning Jane Bull told Thomas that Sir Marcus wished to see him as soon as he had risen. After a pint of porridge, he went to the great hall to wait.

Sir Marcus came in brusquely and told him at once of the events of the day before. Sheriff's men and constables, on a warrant from Sir Marcus and his lawyer Perkins, had marched to Bankside and broken down the door of a former alehouse where John Lynch was believed to lie. There they found stolen goods - mainly clothes, wool and silks and a little plate. The absence of any smaller valuables might be explained by the fact that there was no sign anywhere of Lynch or of his known associates - save a man in a yellow coat who was caught trying to climb out of a window. When Thomas spoke Laughing Morgan's name, Sir Marcus eyed him grimly.

'He's not laughing now, and his name isn't Morgan. He was once a tailor, with a wife and children in the Welsh Borders. Now he's a felon, and he will hang.'

'And Lynch?' Thomas asked, thoughts crowding in upon him.

'I thought you might be able to shed light on his whereabouts,' Sir Marcus answered.

Once again Thomas wondered how much Sir Marcus really knew of this tangled affair. With a shrug he answered: 'Sir, I cannot.'

'We've learned that he has other hiding-places,' Sir Marcus said. 'One is a poor house in Dowgate, but there are others on Bankside. The ward aldermen searched the house in Dowgate but found nothing. As for

Bankside...' he trailed off, with a helpless gesture. In the Stews, everyone knew there were enough places for a man like Lynch to stay hidden for ever.

Thomas chose the moment to tell Sir Marcus about the new gyrfalcons. He abandoned the notion of asking for an extra day: Sir Marcus looked in no mood to grant further favours.

'You may hire a cart and bring the birds here today,' Sir Marcus ordered. 'Place them in the stable. I will sleep soundly in my bed tonight, knowing they are safe within my walls.'

Thomas's mind was busy. This morning when he roused himself, he had made a decision, but he needed time to act.

'Might I have the day to myself sir, to make my preparations?' he asked.

Sir Marcus paused before giving a curt nod of assent. Thomas inclined his head and was about to leave, when the other asked suddenly: 'Where else did you go yesterday, falconer?'

Instinct told him not to speak of the house in Sything Lane. He answered: 'After I spoke with the dealer in hawks, I lost my way. I left the city by Bishopsgate and had to ask directions.'

'You walked all the way back?' Sir Marcus asked. 'Had you not money to return by the river?'

Thomas gave a smile. 'I prefer to walk, Sir Marcus. I'm a man of the open Downs. I dislike boats.'

Sir Marcus grunted, and motioned him to go. Half an hour later, had the knight seen him walk down to the river and take a boat from Whitehall Stairs, he might have wondered at his boldness - or perhaps his impudence. But time was short now, and Thomas had none left to spare.

The morning was chill. The wind now came upriver from the east, so that the watermen cursed and pulled their hat-brims low, heaving against the incoming tide. Thomas asked to be taken to the Tower, which prompted a laugh from the man at the oars.

'What have you done, plotted against the Lord Treasurer?'

Thomas smiled. 'Where I wish to go, is at the far end of the city. I know no other landmark.'

'Where do you seek?' the man asked, between breaths.

'Houndsditch, without the walls.'

The man nodded. 'I'll take you to the bridge, then you must walk by Thames Street as far as Galley Key. There you may cut through Petty Wales and thence to Aldgate by Woodruff Lane and Poor Jewry. Houndsditch is out to your left. You'll know it by the sound of cannon.'

Thomas stared, thinking this was another townsman's joke upon a countryman such as he. But the man went on: 'Cannons are brought from the Tower, to the artillery yard at Spitalfields for practice every Thursday, master. The yard is behind the gun-foundry at Houndsditch.'

Cheerfully he added: 'Best stop up your ears!'

Within the hour, Thomas was walking the entire length of Houndsditch, seeking a house he did not know. And the waterman had spoken truly, for the occasional boom of cannon-fire sounded from across the fields.

He halted halfway along the street, which was almost as busy as any in the city. Here were the shops of the fripperers - the dealers in second-hand clothes, and they were seldom short of custom. Thomas wandered from one open shop-front to another, picking idly at breeches, hats, belts and jerkins as if seeking something in particular. To the annoyance of the shopkeepers who accosted him at every turn, he would not specify what it was. For the best part of two hours he made himself a source of irritation, all the while keeping an eye on the

street. He was half wondering whether he might see a coach driven by a liveried coachman,

though that seemed increasingly unlikely.

Then, as the rumble in his stomach spoke of the approaching hour of dinner, he glanced at the street for the hundredth time, froze and took an involuntary step backwards, colliding with a customer. He apologized, turning quickly to face the shop, his heart thudding.

He had not seen any coach, nor any richly-dressed lady: he had seen John Lynch.

He waited a few seconds, then left the shop and followed, as far behind as he could. He was certain it was he, and not merely because of the short stature and the cropped hair: after facing the man across a table in that stinking room on Bankside, he felt he would know him anywhere.

This time Lynch was alone, and he was in a hurry. Thomas drew a grim satisfaction from the knowledge that his stronghold had been breached the day before, the proceeds of his activities seized, his men scattered. Clearly however, their intelligence network had not failed them, for all had escaped, save Morgan.

Now he might follow Lynch and learn where his hiding place was. But at once, he dismissed the idea: it was no longer part of his scheme. The trail he followed led to Lynch's daughter Susanna. Even if only for his own sake, and whatever the consequences might be, he burned now to discover the truth.

Ahead of him, came the sound of a male voice raised in song, and he saw a crowd spilling across the street. A ballad-singer was busy at his trade: he saw the man, in a bright hat with a feather in it, standing a head taller than those about him, on a little platform of some kind. He sang in a clear, powerful voice. On the edge of the throng, Thomas's sharp eyes also spotted the fellow's accomplice at work. It was an old practice, but an effective one still: the ballad-singer drew the crowd and kept their attention fixed, while the cutpurse relieved them of their money.

But the next moment he cursed himself for letting his own attention wander; Lynch had melted into the crowd.

Thomas pushed his way through, using his height, peering over heads. Clearing the far edge of the noisy crowd, some of whom were joining in with the ballad's chorus, he stood in the middle of the street and looked from left to right. To his relief, he caught sight of a figure disappearing inside the doorway of a house a little way ahead. The door closed, but he was certain the one who had entered was Lynch.

Once again, he had to resign himself to a waiting game. He moved off up the street a little

then walked back, keeping his eyes on the door. The house was three-storeyed, neat and shuttered, with no outward sign of ostentation. It looked like the modest home of a merchant or perhaps of a physician, close enough to the city for business, yet bordering on the open fields without. However, it was doubtful if many would choose such a house for it backed almost on to the gun-foundry, from which came a fearful din of hammers and a grinding of metal.

Thomas had slowed up, passing the house for the fourth time, when the door opened and two men came out. One was a very big, heavy man in black clothes, with thick black hair and a bushy beard. The other, almost a dwarf beside him, was John Lynch.

Thomas turned about and moved to the edge of the crowd, still clustered about the ballad-singer. From there he was able to keep an eye on Lynch, as he walked away from the house without looking back. The big man shouted after him and gestured before going back inside; he had the look of someone who was seeing off an unwelcome intruder.

Thomas moved around the crowd and observed Lynch walk with small, quick steps along Houndsditch, away towards Bishopsgate until he was lost from sight. Then, taking a couple of very deep breaths he crossed the street, walked up to the house and knocked firmly on the heavy door.

Now that he was close he saw that the door was studded with square-headed nails and had a little hatch, barely six inches across, that opened inward at eye-level. It looked indeed, more like the door of a back-street trugging-house than he had expected.

The hatch opened, and a pair of dark eyes peered out at him.

'Whom d'ye seek?' It was a very deep bass voice, with an accent that he did not recognize.

Thomas answered: 'The lady of the house.'

'There be none here,' the voice said, and the eyes drew back.

Before the hatch could be closed, Thomas said: 'It's John Lynch's daughter that I seek. On a matter of importance.'

To his consternation the hatch was shut at once. He waited, then knocked again, looking uneasily about. Further up the street, the ballad-singer had finished his song and the crowd was dispersing. After another moment, the hatch opened and the voice, angry now, barked: 'You do 'ave the wrong 'ouse. If you don't leave the door I will call a constable.'

'Then your mistress will bitterly regret it,' Thomas said, just before the hatch slammed for

what was undoubtedly the last time. Then, his heart in his mouth, he took a step back and waited. After another moment the door half-opened and the giant appeared. With a glare at Thomas, he said: 'State your message, and us'll convey it.'

Thomas shook his head. 'It is for your mistress only to hear.'

The big man paused, giving Thomas a moment in which to observe him. This was no common 'Cerberus' plucked from the door of a Bankside brothel; he had rather the appearance of a wrestler. He was fit and alert, well-poised on the balls of his feet.

It was not fat that hung upon his huge frame, but solid muscle.

'You may wait upon the stoop,' the giant said in his curious accent, 'and no further, while I ask within.'

He drew back, just as a voice called from the house: 'Let no more of them in!'

As the giant half-turned, Thomas took a pace forward and asked: 'Mistress Lynch?'

The light fell on a young woman in a dark frock and fine ruff, descending the stairs rapidly. As she reached the foot of the staircase, Thomas's eyes travelled upwards, and his heart stopped. He was gazing into a face so like that of Lady Margaret, he almost gasped aloud. Instead, he made a quick bow.

At once the giant put a hand out to stay Thomas, but the woman asked sharply: 'Who are you?'

Seizing the moment, he breathed deeply and answered: 'I am a servant to Lady Margaret Vicary.'

She hesitated, then glanced at her bodyguard with the briefest of nods. The man stepped aside, watching Thomas closely, and allowed him to walk in. He was shown into a comfortable parlour at the back, with an oak settle by the chimney-corner, a table and two plain panel-backed chairs. A dish of fruit heaped to a peak sat on the table; there were even portraits on the walls. He stood in the middle of the room, surprised at its homeliness, and waited as the young woman followed him in.

She did not sit nor invite him to do so, but stood close to the doorway, only a few feet from her man-servant. In his deep rolling voice, the giant said: 'I should search 'ee. I don't trust the glaze on 'en.'

He thought he could place the accent. The fellow was from the west country, perhaps a Cornishman.

But he saw now that the young woman appeared agitated. In a low voice she asked: 'How

did you know to come here?'

'Your - ' he almost said father and stopped himself. 'I waited until John Lynch had gone.'

'Why?' she asked, her eyes searching him from head to toe. She had an absent manner, as if

thinking of something other than the business in hand.

'It is a delicate matter, and must be teased out piecemeal,' he began, but the young woman frowned at once.

'State the reason for your visit sir, or I will have my servant throw you out.'

The giant was stooping outside the doorway, his black eyes fixed unwaveringly on Thomas. He had no choice, but to shock her and face the consequences.

'I know of your true parentage,' he said.

The woman did not react. Quietly, he added: 'There are matters to be spoken of in close confidence.'

Again, she said nothing. Looking into her oval face with its near-perfect features, his resolve almost wavered. Though she wore a little paint and powder to whiten her skin, the dark, natural beauty that shone forth would have silenced any man. No wonder, he thought, she was kept here by a rich lord, and guarded like a treasure.

'What do you want of me?' she asked, as sharply as before.

'I want nothing, madam,' he replied. 'It is on Lady Margaret's account that I have come here.'

At this, she lowered her eyes. 'I do not know a Lady Margaret.'

'Yet you would like to, I venture,' he said.

With a sudden, agitated movement of her hands, she turned and spoke softly to the giant, who bent his head to listen. Then looking straight at Thomas, she said: 'This not the hour - nor is it the place. But if you will go to the Theatre in Finsbury Fields at two o'clock, I will meet you.'

That surprised him. As he considered his reply she took a step forwards, pulled a large ring off her finger and held it out.

'Show this token to the gatekeeper, and he will direct you to a private box above the stage. Have you money to pay him?'

He nodded and took the ring without looking closely at it, whereupon she stood aside. The visit was over, but an assignation was to follow. With a bow, Thomas walked from the room followed by the Cornish giant, who barely waited until he had cleared the entrance before slamming the door hard upon him.

In the street, he stood and examined the ring. It was of gold, richly worked, with arabesques of red-enamelled strapwork about a tiny central device. Peering close, he saw that the device was a minute, finely-carved figure of a female nude. Breathing deeply, he started to walk

away, towards Bishopsgate. Cannon-fire still sounded in the distance.

He had a little over an hour to wait until the performance at the Old Theatre, that had now stood for ten years at Shoreditch, north of the city. Crowds poured out of Bishopsgate along Norton Folgate and eastwards from over the fields towards the great round, timbered structure with its

171

circle of three-storeyed seating under a roof of thatch. But Thomas, a newcomer here, stopped in consternation for there were two theatres, surprisingly close together. The one nearer to the city was smaller and meaner, though crowds were thick about its entrance as they were about that of the larger building.

And what crowds; they were of both sexes and most ages, and of every class from richly-dressed nobles to the humblest artisan. Swadders moved here and there with their packs, selling trinkets. From inside came the clamour of an excited audience ripe for the afternoon's entertainment, and above that could be heard the shouts of those that sold bottle-ale and pipes of tobacco. Here and there a painted woman in a low dress and starched ruff made her way through the throng, deaf to the ribald shouts of young prentice-boys at her back. Jostled by the crowd, Thomas stopped a man who from the stench of his balmy jacket must have been a brewer and asked which was the Old Theatre. One or two people within earshot laughed at his ignorance, but the man pointed to the smaller building and said good-humouredly: 'That's the Curtain, master countryman. The farther one's the Theatre.'

At that moment came a loud trumpet-blast from the roof of the Theatre, and the crowd began pushing forward excitedly. Thomas thanked the man and walked on, to mingle with the noisy throng that heaved through the entrance, paying their pennies as they went. But when Thomas drew close to the harassed door-keeper and showed the ring, the man stared at him and said: 'You want the gallery entrance. Round the other side.'

Thomas had to fight his way out the wrong way, through the mass of people that pressed against him. Finally, having shouldered his way clear, he rounded the building to see a thinner and more dignified group filing in through a narrower entrance. Here were the gallants, the gentlemen with their guests, the lords with their ladies spending a day in town - and clearly there were some who came here for meetings of a more discreet nature. For when Thomas showed the token, this gatekeeper nodded in a sly way and directed him to the upper storey, where he should take the last box on the right - and the price here, was sixpence. It seemed that Susanna Lynch had used this place of assignation often enough before.

After paying, Thomas climbed up the narrow wooden stairs and found himself in a thatched gallery high above the stage and the arena, where the groundlings stood crammed together in

all weathers. The gallery opened on to small private boxes, partly shielded from prying eyes

below by a fence of laths. When he entered the last one, which was almost directly above the stage, he found that it was empty.

There was a bench in the box, upholstered in velvet. Uneasily, Thomas seated himself and looked down upon the stage. He had never been to a theatre in his life; the only performances he had seen were on those rare occasions when travelling companies of players had come to Petbury and entertained the household. Sir Robert was a hunting man, with little taste for such indoor pleasures. Lady Margaret however, had delighted in them, Thomas recalled. Now, his pulse quickened at the thought that he was to meet her lost child, her courtesan daughter. He still felt, at times, as if the business of the morning had been but a dream. And here he was in a house of illusions, where nothing was as it seemed; it was fitting. As he tried to order his thoughts, there was a blare of trumpets and a shout from the crowd below: the performance was beginning.

He did not know the name of the play, nor was he in a mind to concentrate on it. Ranting figures jetted forth upon the huge stage, declaiming loudly to make themselves heard above the shouts, laughter, catcalls and general hubbub of the audience. There was a king in rich velvet, who lost his crown and was reduced to pleading for his life before an upstart in black; there was a queen played by a pretty-faced boy in satin, who also sang a song; and there was a clown who popped up at intervals and worked the crowd for all their worth, performing every act of buffoonery possible, from breaking wind to singing lewd rhymes. Thomas watched silently from his high perch, his mind elsewhere. For as the afternoon wore on it was becoming more and more plain that his assignation had failed: the beautiful young courtesan did not appear.

Anxiously he watched the door, then took to scanning faces in other boxes, and even in the crowd below, but there was no sign of Susanna Lynch. Some of the ladies in the boxes, he noticed, wore masks; but when he looked at them he immediately found himself glared at by some gentleman or other, and looked away. As the performance ended with a song and a roll of drums, he rose from his seat and went out.

Behind him, the crowd roared and applauded, and the music of the jig that would follow the play began at once, but Thomas paid it no heed. He descended the stairs, hurried out into the muddy lanes of Shoreditch, and walked swiftly back towards Bishopsgate. Turning into Houndsditch, he reached Susanna Lynch's house, just as the door opened and a man appeared on the step before him.

It was the lawyer, Nicholas Stocker.

CHAPTER 16

For a brief interval the two men stared in amazement at one another. Then a look of annoyance appeared on Stocker's face. In an icy tone, he asked: 'Still meddling, falconer?'

In Thomas's mind, something clicked into place. Returning the man's gaze, he countered: 'Is Mistress Lynch at home? I have matters to discuss with her.'

'The lady of the house is not here,' Stocker said. Pulling his gown about him he started to brush past Thomas, who got the sudden impression that something was amiss. The lawyer was in too much of a hurry.

'Won't you stay, sir?' Thomas asked, and put a hand on the man's arm. 'I believe if we traded our intelligence, we would both learn much.'

But Stocker swept his arm away and took a pace into the street, whereupon Thomas gripped the edge of his fur-trimmed gown and asked: 'Is there any message you would like me to convey to Lady Margaret?'

Irritably Stocker tried to pull his cloak away, but Thomas held it fast. A passer-by glanced at the two men but kept on walking.

'May we go inside and talk for a minute?' Thomas persisted.

'You insolent devil,' Stocker snapped. 'I could have you arrested.'

Thomas gave him a thin smile. 'Would that be wise? When you have drawn so much attention to yourself already?'

Stocker flicked his head in an agitated manner, and said: 'Let me go at once, or I'll have you clapped up in Newgate.'

At that moment, from within the house, came a terrible cry; a drawn-out expression of agony.

Stocker ripped his cloak from Thomas's grasp and stepped away, but Thomas took his arm, twisted it and bent it quickly behind his back, then whirled him about to face the open door. Stocker hissed with pain. Without another word Thomas marched him into the house.

Another sound, more like a deep groan, drew him to the doorway at his left. Pushing the unwilling Stocker before him, he entered a room that was barely-furnished - and saw a deep red pool, spreading across the floor towards him. Against the far wall sat the Cornish giant, white-faced and motionless, his body from the chest downwards soaked with blood.

Involuntarily Thomas loosened his grip on Stocker. At once the lawyer tore himself away, turning from the sickening sight, and tried to get out. But Thomas stepped sideways and blocked his way.

'You run from here, and I'll swear to all London you did this.'

Stocker's face showed white. 'I do not wear a sword!'

Ignoring him, Thomas crossed the room and knelt on one knee beside the giant.

'Can you talk?' he asked.

The man opened his eyes and gazed at him. He was close to death.

'They can't fight like true men,' he said softly. 'But rim me through with rapiers.'

'Was it Lynch?' Thomas asked. The man only stared at him. Then he gave a low groan and coughed a little.

'Did they take her?' Thomas asked urgently. But there was no answer. A bubble of blood appeared on the giant's lips.

There was a sound from behind. Thomas looked round quickly, expecting to find Stocker gone. But he was still there, leaning against the door-frame. He wore a sickly smile.

'Of course they took her, you fool,' he said.

Thomas looked hard at him. 'You were acting for her, not for Nathaniel Pickering.'

A sneer spread over Stocker's pale face. 'You know nothing, falconer. Stick to your craft, would be my advice.'

Just then the giant gave a low moan and Thomas turned back quickly. The man's breath was very slow and weak. Thomas spoke close to his ear.

'I'll do whatever I can for her. I swear it.'

A look of anxiety came over the broad face. Thomas watched with pity; he could find no words of comfort. The dark eyes wandered for a moment, then fixed upon him.

'I did mortally love 'er,' he said, and died.

Thomas walked outside, leaned his arm against the heavy front door and took a few deep breaths.

Stocker had followed. 'Satisfied now, falconer?' he said in a bitter voice. Thomas ignored him.

'If you will let me pass,' Stocker continued, with an attempt at imperiousness, 'I have business elsewhere.'

Thomas turned on him. 'Not before you tell me where Lynch has taken her,' he said.

'I do not know anyone called Lynch,' the lawyer began, but Thomas had no patience left.

Pushing him back against the door-frame, he said: 'I'll spill everything I know of this matter to Sir Marcus Brooke. His lawyer - Doctor Perkins - seemed most interested in your

involvement in Lady Margaret's affairs.'

Stocker's eyes rolled upwards. When he spoke again, it was almost a splutter. 'I'll have you killed within two days.'

'Like they killed Nathaniel?'

'I was not involved in that!' he shouted. 'I deplored it!'

Now, they had drawn the attention of the street. Several people stopped to stare, and a man called out; 'Here's a fight!'

Thomas let go of Stocker and turned to the small crowd that was gathering. 'Call the constables,' he said. 'There's a fellow been killed in this house.'

There was a gasp. Someone called: 'Is that the murderer?'

Without expression, Thomas turned back to Stocker. His face was haggard.

'What shall it be, master lawyer?' Thomas whispered to him. 'Do you tell me where Lynch has taken her, or do I keep you here until the constables arrive?'

Stocker began to speak softly and rapidly. 'There's a reward beyond your dreams, falconer, there for the taking if you'll but listen. She has powerful connections - the highest.'

'Lynch,' Thomas said. 'Where has he taken her?'

'Listen to your heart,' Stocker said, with a grotesque attempt at a smile. 'You and I can act in consort - Lynch can hang, and all his dogs with him... we shall reap riches!'

The crowd was growing, pressing closer, muttering. A large woman in a cap pushed through to the front and announced: 'My husband's under-constable of Holywell. I've sent word for him.'

Stocker tried to wrench himself away, but Thomas gripped his arm and held on, whispering: 'I'll keep your name out of it, if you'll help me to Lynch.'

Stocker looked quickly about. All eyes were upon him. He spoke from the side of his mouth. 'Go to the Bear Garden, on Bankside. Ask for Edward Mace.'

Thomas dropped his arm in pure surprise. In an instant Stocker stepped into the street and would have hurried away, but the crowd surged about him. A sturdy man in a leather apron laid a hand on his shoulder and asked: 'Where to so quickly, master?'

'Let me go!' Stocker shouted. 'I am a lawyer!'

There was a murmur from the crowd. Stocker began to panic, struggling to free himself. Wild-eyed, he turned back towards the house and shouted: 'You have ruined me, falconer! I will make you pay - if I live!'

Then he stopped, with a man gripping him by either arm, and stared up the street. Thomas had gone.

He had no time left to waste. He half-walked, half-ran, along Houndsditch and entered the city again by Aldgate. Retracing his steps of the morning, he hurried through Crutched Friars, then by Mart Lane to Tower Street. Following the sounds of the river, he found his way to the Keys and in minutes arrived once again at van Velsen's shop in Botolph Key. Without waiting, he pushed his way through a group of customers and found the Dutchman.

'My friend.' Van Velsen broke into a ready smile. 'All is ready for you.' He indicated a wicker travelling-cage. Recovering his breath, Thomas suddenly remembered that he was supposed to collect the falcons.

Seeing the look on his face, the Dutchman's smile faded. Thomas took him aside, and told him that the ones who killed the falcons had escaped the law, but he had found out where they were. If the Dutchman could gather some men together they could go now, across the river to

179

Bankside.

Van Velsen's face was a blank. Slowly he lowered his eyes, and Thomas followed them down to his own boots, which were stained with blood from the room where the giant had died. As if picking up the scent, the birds in the nearest cages all began screeching at once.

'They have killed one man today,' Thomas said quietly. 'I watched him die. Come with me and help me find them.'

After a moment, the Dutchman nodded.

An hour later, as the afternoon waned, Thomas crossed London Bridge with van Velsen and half a dozen other Dutch artisans from the eastern end of London. Some carried clubs, others billhooks, one even had a hammer. Most had poniards. Van Velsen himself carried a butcher's knife, and a poniard at his belt.

The crowds on the bridge parted, watching them curiously as they tramped southwards and emerged in a body from the Great Stone Gate, beneath the pikes from which leered the grisly heads of executed traitors. Turning sharply to the right, they marched through muddy lanes past St Mary Overies and crossed the rickety bridge over the brook by Dead Man's Place. Here, on the Bishop of Winchester's land, they were outside the city's authority in Bankside, the home of lawlessness and pleasure. Noise came from taverns, gaming-houses, alehouses and brothels. People here stood and watched warily, as the determined group of men walked up to a circular, theatre-like structure, but one with a very different purpose from that of putting on plays.

The day's sport being over this late in the afternoon, the Bear Garden was eerily quiet. On the right, sounds of revelry came from the Bankside shore where the Stews faced the river.

Before them the houses gave way to fields dotted with trees; another circular structure, the Bull Ring, was visible further along, but it too was quiet. To their left were a pond and rows of kennels where the mastiffs were housed. At once, the ferocious dogs set up a menacing chorus of barks.

The doors of the Garden stood wide open, but it was empty. Thomas, his face set grimly, banged on the rough-hewn timbers and shouted.

A roughly-dressed man appeared from around the corner of an outhouse adjoining the Bear Garden. Confronted by what was clearly a hostile group, he stopped some distance away. Then, in a voice that Thomas knew at once, he called: 'The Garden is closed now, masters. Come Sunday, and you shall have fine sport - five dogs to be set against t' biggest bear!'

The Dutchmen, some of whom were tall and all of whom were stout, stood in silence. But Thomas walked forward, saying: 'Master Mace. Remember me?'

The bearward frowned, then recognition dawned. Taking a step towards Thomas, he said with controlled anger: 'You got Ben Stubbs killed, falconer.' Then he gripped his right earlobe and pulled it forward. 'And you got me this.'

A neat hole, crimson at the edges, had been burned through his ear; the usual punishment for a second conviction for vagrancy. Mace had paid for his involvement in Nathaniel Pickering's death.

'If what I now believe is true,' Thomas answered him, 'you were lucky not to hang.'

Anger smouldered in the bearward's eyes. He had not the air of innocence he wore that day he stood in the coroner's court at Petbury.

'And working at the Bear Pit does not sicken you quite so much after all,' Thomas added.

The tension was growing. The Dutchmen moved towards Edward Mace, hefting their weapons. But Mace stood his ground and waited. A memory flashed up before Thomas, of that fair day on the Downs when he had first seen the man, puffing uphill after his bear. He did not want to believe that Mace was involved in any of Lynch's business. And yet:

'Were you part of it?' he asked shortly. 'Were you supposed to let your bear rend him, to make it look like an accident?'

Mace returned his gaze steadily. 'I told truth,' he replied. 'Horseman was already dead. I just

moved t' body off road.'

Stepping closer, Thomas said: 'But you know who killed him.'

Mace said nothing.

'Was it Cook?' Thomas asked. Behind him, he felt van Velsen stiffen like a post. On the

way, he had told him the name of the one whose earring had been torn off by the falcon.

'Go to t' devil,' Mace said suddenly.

Van Velsen took a step towards him. From within the outhouse, came the sound of a large animal, stamping and growling.

'We want Cook, and we want John Lynch,' Thomas said.

There were footsteps. Mace was smiling now. 'We'd been told to expect company,' he said.

Thomas turned to see four or five men appear from around the side of the Bear Garden. The Dutchmen turned too, as a low door in the thick timbered wall opened, and several more men stepped out. Leading them was Cook, Lynch's strong man, the killer of the falcons whose face still bore the marks of his crime.

There was a moment of silence, then someone gave a shout, and

Lynch's ruffians formed a semi-circle. As the Dutchmen turned to face them, with the open gates of the Bear Garden at their backs, Thomas realized that in his heart he had known it would come down to this. There was no law to help them here; it was one body of men against another, and there were no rules.

But soon it became evident that Lynch's men had some purpose in mind. They came forward in a skirmish line, swinging clubs, axe-handles and staves, driving Thomas and the others backwards through the gates into the arena, towards the heavy stake in its centre to which hapless animals were tied for baiting. Cook had a sword and was the undisputed leader. He came on boldly while Edward Mace, in the rear, closed the heavy doors and bolted them.

Lynch's people wanted no witnesses, nor did they intend to let any of their foes escape; it would be a fight for survival. And had there been spectators there that evening, they would no doubt have set up a roar as loud as any heard on Bankside, because on this occasion the combatants were not dumb beasts, but men.

Mutterings on both sides gave to shouts, then to actions, but Thomas had no opportunity to look to his companions, for a thick-set fellow wielding a cudgel was bearing down upon him with a snarl worthy of the surroundings. Thomas ducked as the man swung his weapon, then

came up with his fists whirling. The left caught the man on the chin, checking him long enough for Thomas to drive a right into the middle of his face. The man stopped dead, blood welling from his nose. In surprise at the ease with which he had stunned his opponent, Thomas yanked the cudgel from the man's hand and banged him over the head. The fellow went down and stayed there.

For now it became clear that not all of these men were proficient fighters. Some of them were no more than tavern loafers, eager no doubt for the purse Lynch had promised them. But Cook and one or two others were of sterner mettle. Among them, Thomas had noticed by now, were his assailant in the Spanish jerkin, from that day he had taken a beating in the alley, and his scowling companion. Each of them fought viciously against the Dutchmen, who were defending themselves courageously but with some desperation. Everywhere now men were grappling in pairs, hand to hand, or swinging clubs at each other. As Thomas whirled about, seeking where he could be of some use, he saw one of the Dutchmen fall on his back, with the jerkined ruffian standing over him. The man raised his club to deal a skull-cracking blow.

But Thomas had the cudgel. In a second, he had gained the short distance between himself and the other, swinging the weapon with all his strength. The force of the blow knocked the fellow off his feet. As he hit the ground with a cry, Thomas swung the cudgel again and caught him on the forehead. The crack was audible over the shouts, curses and yells of pain that now resounded all about the amphitheatre. The man slumped in a heap.

So the battle raged, with men grievously hurt on both sides. Some were stabbed with poniards, and lay bleeding, crying out in rage and agony. Others were lying stunned or unconscious on the packed earth floor, that had been stained with the blood of decades. It soon dawned on Lynch's people, that they had badly underestimated their opponents. Fuelled by a righteous anger, these stout Dutch working-men, who had survived war and persecution in the Low Countries before settling in England, were not inclined to turn tail and run. Van Velsen, strong as a bull, crushed one man until his ribs cracked, then turned and grappled with another who bore down on him with an axe-handle. The handle caught him on the shoulder, but the Dutchman had brought his butcher's knife up. Even as he sagged under the blow, he thrust the weapon forward into his assailant's shoulder. The man screamed and leaped back, dropping his weapon and staring at the blood which pumped through his clothing. He sat down, still staring, and stayed seated while the fight raged on about him. Thomas fought desperately, the way he had once done in the same land from which his companions hailed, because once again he could do no other. The furore of that battlefield, with its noise and its scent of fear, rose up before him, a memory he hated. But now his anger rose when he turned from knocking one more rogue to the ground and saw the face of Cook the killer approaching him at speed. Dropping the cudgel, Thomas pulled his poniard from his belt, but the next second it was swept from his hand by a side-swipe of Cook's sword.

Backing away towards the wall of the arena, Thomas looked into the man's sweating face and saw the death-lust in his eyes. With a half-grin, intent on his purpose, the man raised his sword. He did not see the figure that appeared suddenly behind him, but Thomas looked over Cook's shoulder, long enough for him to realize the danger. As he spun round, he ducked swiftly, and van Velsen's butcher knife missed its target. The next second, Cook's sword had slashed the Dutchman across the arm. He staggered backwards, as Cook whirled about to face Thomas again. But that brief second was all Thomas had needed to change his position. Cook swung his sword, but Thomas swerved aside and the man lost his balance. Then, knowing he had but the one chance, Thomas leaned in, gripped the man's sword-arm and twisted it with all his strength.

But Cook did not let go; nor did he intend to lose the fight. He slammed a fist into Thomas's jaw, then an elbow into his stomach. As Thomas doubled up in pain, Cook wrenched his arm free and took a step backwards, raising his sword for the kill.

Through a haze, Thomas watched the weapon glint in the air above him for what seemed like minutes, then start to fall. As it did so, there was a harsh scream from Cook, who toppled forwards, knocking Thomas flat to the ground, and lay prostrate across his chest.

Thomas lay stunned, as Cook's heavy body kept him pinned to the ground, even as it twitched in its death-throes. Then someone leaned over him and rolled the body off. Struggling to a sitting position, he saw the knife sticking at an angle out of Cook's lower back beside his spine, and a white-faced van Velsen, blood running from his sleeve, standing beside him, breathing heavily.

Winded, Thomas got slowly to his feet. Looking about, he saw now that every one of Lynch's men was on the ground. Some of the Dutchmen were hurt, two of them badly, but none was killed. With relief, he eyed van Velsen.

'You saved my life.'

Van Velsen jerked his head towards Cook's lifeless body. 'I avenge falcons,' he said.

At that moment, the sound of bolts being drawn made them look round. Edward Mace had got to his feet unnoticed, opened the low door in the wall and was about to escape.

Thomas picked up Cook's sword and ran across the scuffed floor of the Bear Garden. As he reached the door it was swung shut in his face, but he wrenched it open and pushed his way through, to see Mace disappearing round the corner of the outhouse.

Rounding the low building, Thomas skidded to a halt. There stood Mace, breathless and bruised, with a heavy chain in his hand - his favoured weapon. From the bolted door of the outhouse, came the roaring of his bear.

'Take one step, falconer, and I'll turn 'im loose,' he panted, and put a hand on the door-bolt.

'There's a sworn warrant for the arrest of Lynch and all his fellows,' Thomas said quickly. 'You want to join them in Newgate? It'll be the gallows tree this time.'

Mace snorted. 'You're too late. Lynch is gone.'

'Leaving the rest of you to your fate?' Thomas asked. 'What price loyalty, master bearward?'

The man glared, and Thomas pressed him. 'If you show me the house where he has taken the lady, I'll turn my back long enough for you to lose yourself.'

Mace looked non-plussed. 'Taken t' lady?'

'Susanna Lynch,' Thomas said. 'Don't pretend you don't know who she is.'

'She's not a lady,' Mace sneered. 'She's nobbut a bawd.'

'Tell me where she is,' Thomas said, and raised the sword.

Something in his expression quelled Mace's defiance. With a jerk of his head, he said: 'She's in Heaven.'

For a second, Thomas misunderstood. Then he remembered the same words being spoken to him in a bare room by a skinny little trull, only two days ago.

'Where's Heaven?' he asked.

'Yonder,' Mace answered, and pointed towards Bankside. 'With all t' other pick-hatches.'

'She's a prisoner, then,' Thomas said, and started forward. But Mace gave a harsh laugh.

'Prisoner? She owns t' place.'

Then he turned and ran away.

CHAPTER 17

Thomas walked back into the Bear Garden. The Dutchmen were tending their wounded, bandaging cuts and fashioning makeshift crutches and splints. From the nearby kennels, dogs still barked. The fight had of course attracted attention, and it would be wise to leave quickly. Any representatives of the law who eventually turned up were unlikely to make distinctions, but would lump all the participants together.

'You come with us?' van Velsen asked him.

Thomas shook his head. 'My business is not yet finished here.'

Outside the doors of the arena, ignoring the stares of a few onlookers, he asked: 'Will you and your friends be safe?'

Van Velsen nodded. 'The dead man, we will throw in the river. Nobody question us - all Dutchmen alike, to them.'

Thomas handed him Cook's sword. 'You can sell this for a goodly sum. It'll go some way towards compensating you for your losses.'

'You come tomorrow, for falcons?' van Velsen asked.

Only now, did Thomas remember that he was supposed to leave the next day. 'Can you have them delivered early in the morning, to Sir Marcus Brooke's house on the Strand?' he asked.

The Dutchman nodded. 'You go home now, to country?'

Thomas smiled. 'London's a little too warm for my taste.' He put out a hand, and van Velsen gripped it firmly.

'You come and visit again, my friend. We drink, talk of this.'

'I would be glad to,' Thomas answered.

Then he walked away, around the corner towards Bankside.

He found Heaven easily enough. There were stout railings about it, and spikes on the gate through which he had been marched by Lynch's men. Yet despite the grim facade, it was clearly a house of pleasure. The door was open, and beside it stood the huge black Cerberus, in the same sleeveless jerkin and scarlet cap.

The dusk was falling, and lights showed at the windows. Thomas was swearing borrowed clothes, and had done his best to straighten his appearance, yet he was afraid of being recognized. However, the livid scar on his cheek must have altered his appearance considerably, because the big man merely stood in his way and growled: 'Whom do you seek, master?'

As brightly as he could, Thomas answered: 'I've had good fortune at the tables, my friend, and have guineas to spend. Will you make a man welcome here, at bawdy-banquet?'

The man looked him over with a sceptical smile. 'Good fortune, you say?' He gave a throaty laugh.

Thomas laughed in turn. 'You mean the scar? Let's say one fellow was less than willing to pay up. I had to persuade him.'

The man still barred his way. After a moment he held out a huge hand and made a rubbing motion between thumb and forefinger.

'Garnish for the doorkeeper sir,' he said.

With relief Thomas dug into his purse, pulled out a sixpence and dropped it into the man's palm. With a broad grin, he stood aside.

'Pray enter Heaven,' he said, then turned and clapped his hands. As Thomas stepped past him into the dimly-lit passage a small, slim figure appeared before him. To his alarm, he found himself staring at the young drab from the upstairs room where he had been held, just two days ago.

'You!' she cried, her eyes wide with recognition. 'You broke my mirror!'

Dipping into his purse quickly, he found a threepence. 'That's for a new one, as I promised,' he said.

The girl broke at once into a childish smile of pleasure.

'Then you are a gentleman, and no stale rogue,' she said, taking the coin quickly. 'Will it please you to enter?'

Thomas followed her along the passage. When they reached the foot of the staircase he stopped and asked: 'Will you take me to your mistress? Susanna Lynch, I mean.'

The girl's smile vanished. 'Am I not good enough to serve you?'

'Later,' he said. 'I have business first with your mistress.'

At that she pouted. 'Dame Bawd's in her parlour and has left word she is not to be disturbed.'

Thomas glanced about him, whereupon the girl drew back in alarm. 'I should be beaten if I disobey,' she said.

He brought out another threepence. 'Show me to her door,' he said, 'and I shall not tell it was you.'

She hesitated, then took the money and led the way to the back of the house. From upstairs came sounds of laughter and revelry.

The girl stopped outside a door, pointed, then hurried away. Thomas raised a hand to knock, then lowered it. The uncertainty he had felt on first meeting Susanna Lynch was as nothing to the confusion he now felt; he no longer knew what to believe. For a moment, he was tempted to turn and walk out. Instead he took a deep breath, gripped the latch, and thrust the door open.

It was a bare room, with few comforts. She was sitting at a small table, in the act of raising a goblet to her lips. As he walked in she lowered it, frowned and would have uttered some word of reproof, but then she recognized him.

There was a pause, during which he closed the door behind him and leaned against it. 'You were not at the theatre,' he said.

Putting the goblet on the table, she stood up slowly. Once again, he saw Lady Margaret; in the tall, well-proportioned figure, the face, even the manner. Now she wore a low-cut russet gown and a lot of jewellery, which reminded him of the ring she had given him. He fished in his pocket and drew it out.

'I came also to return this,' he added, and threw it on to the table.

At last she spoke. 'What do you want of me?'

'I thought rather, it was you who might want something of me.'

She put on a contemptuous look. 'What in heaven's name could you have, that I would want?'

He was tired and sore, and the thought of a verbal fencing-match now was more than he could stomach. Coming away from the door, he said: 'Let me speak. Then, if nothing I say is of use to you, I will go away and leave you be.'

She looked him up and down. 'You have been in a fight, sir.'

'John Lynch's men are beaten,' he told her. 'A warrant is sworn for his arrest. I know he had my lady's brother killed. I also know you have bought up Nathaniel Pickering's debts, and his house. And I have an idea why.'

After a moment, she sat down. Without waiting for an invitation he sat down heavily in a chair opposite her, and said: 'I believe you are Lady Margaret's child, born before her marriage.'

She said nothing.

'I also believe you did not wish for this campaign against her, but that

192

it was Lynch's

scheme, to intimidate her ladyship, or—'

She gave a short, bitter laugh. 'Envy is what drives him. That and a thirst for vengeance,

against the Pickerings - and against me.'

'Vengeance for what?' Thomas asked.

'For what I have become, without his help... and for what I will not do, for him.'

'What is that?' he asked.

She looked coldly at him. 'These are my affairs, sir. I will not discuss them with you.'

He pressed her. 'When you did not come, I went back to your house. Nicholas Stocker was there. He said they had carried you here, by force.' He paused. 'The constables were called in. They will have found the... your servant.'

She looked away. When she turned back, he saw to his surprise that she was distressed.

'Is he dead?' she asked.

He nodded. 'He had lost much blood. I watched him die.'

Her clear eyes filled with tears. With candour, he said:

'You are the unlikeliest bawd I have ever seen.'

At that she sniffed, wiped her eyes and snapped: 'You know nothing of me, sir. And you have nothing to trade.'

'Perhaps not,' he answered. 'Yet it was my mistress, Lady Vicary, who first set me to find you.'

She started, but recovered quickly. 'She does not know me.'

'No,' he agreed. 'But she had begun to believe that her child was not dead, as she had once been told.'

She got up then, agitated as she had been that morning. She began speaking quickly, almost to herself.

'Now I cannot go back, for they have ruined all. My Lord must take care of it. He will fear a scandal... he will be angry.'

She banged a hand down on the table, with surprising force. 'I pulled myself from the mire and rose high enough to pour scorn upon them all. When John Lynch found me, I spat on him... that coward, that greedy, drunken javel... if he had only let me stay as I was!'

'A rich man's plaything,' Thomas said.

Rounding on him she cried: 'That would have been enough! To know that Lynch was not my father would have been enough, too... but more, I learn that the knock-kneed callet whose heels I dogged for the first ten years of my life, is not my mother. My mother is a lady... a lady of wealth and beauty - and I am her daughter and can never know her!'

He was surprised how readily she had lowered her guard; she did not seem to care whether

he heard her or not. Bitterly she went on: 'I thought to confront her - to demand, if not her name, then at least her recognition. Now, everything has gone amiss - because of him.'

He leaned forward and asked quietly: 'What of your father?'

She was suddenly suspicious. 'What is he to you?'

'They say he was a Catholic priest. A Spaniard.'

She frowned. 'Who says so?'

Carefully, he answered: 'That is why her ladyship's brother chose to blackmail her. He alone knew her secret.'

But she shook her head. 'Not he alone. My fa-' she stopped and corrected herself impatiently. 'John Lynch knew.'

'And tried to blackmail you?'

She laughed harshly. 'You think I would let him? One word to my Lord, and Lynch would be crushed like a gnat.'

He recalled suddenly, Matthew Selden's words to him: 'He would swat you like a fly.' The memory stirred his feelings.

'Men have died because of your secret, madam,' he said.

She looked down at him, and suddenly he felt her anger, hard as iron, bent upon his. She wielded a power of her own. Lynch would indeed have been no match for her in the end.

'Have a care you do not become one of them,' she said.

He ignored the threat and continued. 'Still, Lynch dared to come back to your house, and take you away.'

She almost snorted. 'He did not! I chose to come here. I have many houses.'

He looked her in the eye; how wrong he had been about her.

'Where s Lynch?' he asked abruptly.

'In one of his bolt-holes,' she answered. 'He knew he was followed. He ran like a rabbit.'

'And left his cut-throats to bear the brunt.'

She shrugged to show she cared nothing for them. A silence fell, but he had seen a way forward. He would try it, at least.

'If you would like to meet with your - with Lady Margaret,' he said, 'in secret of course - I might perhaps, be permitted to arrange it.'

She sat down slowly. 'You are but a servant.'

'I am her falconer,' he said, as if remembering it himself. 'I enjoy her trust. We sometimes ride alone together for hours, far away from her home, at Petbury.'

There was a moment, then with a knowing look she remarked:

'That would indeed imply a great measure of trust. On the lady's part, as well as on that of her husband.'

Try as he might, Thomas could not prevent the flush that rose to his face.

Susanna Lynch smiled. 'Do not fret, master falconer; your secret is safe in my hands. Perhaps we may trade after all.'

Her whole expression had changed. The effect was dazzling, so that Thomas looked away. She was harsh, even cruel, and old beyond her years, yet her beauty robbed him of speech.

Then she spoke bitterly. 'Yet, she will not want to see me.'

'I will wager that she does,' he replied.

She stared into the distance, then murmured: 'I would dearly love to speak with her, about the father.'

'Her father? Master Pickering?'

'No! My father.'

Thomas watched her keenly. 'You do not know who he is?'

She returned his stare, without expression. 'You ask too many questions of me.'

She stood, and picking up the ring from the table, said: 'I will send this token to you, with news of where I can be found. If she will meet me, send word and I will be ready.'

She waited until he rose. A spell seemed to have been broken. Outside it would be dark; he would have to return and explain himself once again, to Sir Marcus.

'Lynch-' he began, but she shook her head vehemently.

'If he has any wits left, he will flee London and go back to the road, to the vagrom life. He was a ruffler, a mean sort of prince himself, and should have kept to his station. As a leader of thieves and cut-throats, he failed.'

He turned to go and almost bowed, forgetting that he was in a Bankside brothel, and his hostess no more than a bawd. At this she laughed slightly and said: 'My Lord has taught me to behave like a lady, falconer. Even though I am his best-kept secret.'

Then she added: 'You have not told me your name.'

'Thomas Finbow,' he said, and walked outside. As she followed him into the passage, the young drab appeared from nowhere, and said in a whining voice: 'He did force his way in, madam. I could not gainsay him.'

Thomas looked down at her, then said to Susanna: 'I have a daughter, little younger than she.'

'Then be sure you raise her with more care than this one had,' she answered, and turned away.

Under the watchful eyes of the gatekeeper, he passed through the door of Heaven, and out into the night.

It was late when Thomas returned at last to Sir Marcus's house. The gates were locked, and an elderly serving-man appeared, in an ill temper. Opening the gate an inch he peered at Thomas, then snapped:

'It was believed you were gone away again, falconer.'

Too tired to make reply, Thomas followed him inside and soon entered the familiar warmth of the kitchen. The household had nearly all gone to bed, and the room was deserted. Thomas sank into a chair at the long table, whereupon the man promptly retired, leaving him to his own devices.

Despite his exhaustion, sleep seemed a distant prospect. He sat staring through the window at the great houses along the river, black against the starlit sky. He had learned much this long day; if there was more, he no longer wanted to know it. Tomorrow he could leave for Petbury with the falcons, as arranged, and Sir Marcus need not know every detail of his adventure. He would be home with Eleanor at last, and he would try to explain his actions to Sir Robert. That would be difficult, but he had an important ally in Lady Margaret. He believed that once he had told her everything, she would help him. At least, he might be allowed to keep his position as falconer. Of the other matter - the night they had spent together, upstairs in this house - he dared not think. He had a nagging fear that in the intervening days, which now seemed long, she might somehow have turned against him as Sir Robert had.

The back door opened then. He turned quickly to see Jane Bull entering with her keys, a cloak about her shoulders. She saw him at once and stopped in her tracks. Then she noticed his dishevelled appearance. He gave her a tired smile.

'Don't fret,' he said. 'I can shift for myself this time.'

She turned and locked the door, then came towards him. For a moment, she looked angry with him. But he stood up slowly and took her in an embrace. Rather fiercely, she kissed him on the mouth, then leaned back and said: 'What in heaven's name shall I do with you, Thomas?'

He shrugged. 'You will not be troubled much longer. I must leave early tomorrow.'

She gave him a wan look, and said: 'Mayhap I should follow James's example, and ask Sir

Marcus to let me go to Petbury.' Before he could reply, she gave a short laugh. 'Does that not alarm you?'

He touched her cheek tenderly. 'Should it?'

She looked around the kitchen, then moved away from him, but let her hand fall into his. 'If I wake you early enough,' she said softly, 'not even Lady Alice will suspect us.'

He allowed her to lead him towards the stairs.

In the chill of a grey autumn morning, Thomas saddled the good black horse Sir Marcus had provided and prepared to take his leave. About nine o'clock a carter arrived with the cage containing the two gyrfalcons, which caused quite a stir in the stable-yard. Sir Marcus himself insisted on coming down from his breakfast to take a look at them.

'A handsome pair of birds, falconer,' he said. 'You were fortunate to find such.'

The falcons had been well-fed and looked contented enough. Thomas had put hay in the cage and found a cloth to cover it.

Sir Marcus glanced towards the house, where the face of Lady Alice had appeared at an upstairs window. He waved cheerfully, until his wife moved away, then turned to Thomas and spoke in an undertone.

'I thought it best to conduct our conversation out here.'

Thomas nodded politely. Inwardly, he was on his guard at once.

'I would like a full account of your whereabouts yesterday,' Sir Marcus went on. Then rather brusquely, he added: 'But perchance, you would prefer not to make it too full.'

Standing beside the horse, which stamped a foot impatiently, Thomas hesitated, then told of the fight at the Bear Garden.

'Is John Lynch taken?' Sir Marcus asked.

'No, sir. Though his men are beaten and scattered on Bankside, and one was killed. The one who killed the falcons.'

Sir Marcus drew a breath. 'Did you kill him?'

'No, sir. Though I had a part in it.'

'Do you know aught of the lawyer? Doctor Stocker?'

'He...' Thomas sought for tire right words. 'He will no longer be a threat to Lady Margaret, I am certain of it.'

'And what of you, falconer?' Sir Marcus asked, suddenly leaning closer. 'Are you a threat?'

'To whom, Sir Marcus?' Thomas asked.

'To your mistress, to Sir Robert - to anyone,' the other retorted. 'Am I to trust you, that is

what I must know.'

'Be assured sir,' Thomas answered carefully, 'that I would do anything I could to be returned to my master's service. And would serve him, and Lady Margaret, faithfully thereafter.'

'Indeed,' Sir Marcus said drily. 'You would be very wise, to follow such a course.'

He took a sealed document from his pocket and handed it to him. 'There is the letter for Sir Robert, as I promised. Now you must start on your journey.'

Thomas took the letter with a short bow, and Sir Marcus turned to go. But first he paused and said: 'When you and I meet in future, it will be at hawking. We shall not have occasion to converse again as we have done here - ever. Do you understand?'

Thomas nodded. 'I wish to offer you my thanks, sir.'

Sir Marcus snorted. 'Take good care of that gelding,' he said, and stalked off towards the house.

Watched by a groom, Thomas strapped the wicker cage on to the horse, then returned to the kitchen to collect his cloak. Jane Bull was waiting for him.

'There's bread and cheese for your journey,' she said, and handed him a cloth-wrapped package. 'And a sweet apple.'

She walked outside with him. Aware that they were both being observed, they were abrupt in their farewell. But as he stood beside the horse to tie his bundle to the straps, she leaned close and whispered: 'If you return, I shall be here.'

'I wish to God that I might,' he answered. Then he swung himself up into the saddle, shook the reins, and rode out of the yard without looking back.

CHAPTER 18

Late the next afternoon, Thomas rode up the windswept lane to Petbury. October was on the wane; the leaves had turned and a strong westerly wind, fresh off the Atlantic, swept from the Downs. He had felt it for the last ten miles, and it gave him hope. When he clattered into the cobbled yard and dismounted stiffly, a groom appeared in the stable doorway. It was James.

'By the Lord, Thomas,' he said, coming forward in surprise. 'We'd almost given you up for lost.'

Thomas nodded to him and stood loosening the saddle-girth. Gripping his arm, James added: 'But I am mighty glad to see you.'

'I hope you're not the only one who is,' Thomas answered. 'Will you tend to the horse? He has served me well.'

'I don't doubt that,' James said, taking the reins from him. 'This is Actaeon - one of Sir Marcus's best mounts.' He gazed at Thomas. 'What in God's name have you been about?'

Thomas gave a shrug. 'What of you? How fares Catherine?' The groom broke into a grin. 'We are to be married. Sir Robert has given his consent, and I'm the happiest man in Petbury.'

Thomas gave him a smile, then untied the cage in which the two falcons had spent a bumpy but peaceful enough ride. Telling James he would return for the birds later, he went directly to the house. More than anything else, he wanted to see Eleanor; but first he thought he had better find Martin the steward. To say that he was uncertain of the warmth of his reception, would have been something of an understatement.

Less than a quarter of an hour later, Thomas stood cap in hand in the great hall, before a surprisingly subdued Sir Robert Vicary. Instead of pacing before the fire with his usual energy, the knight sat in a carved chair, staring at the floor.

He listened while Thomas told his tale. Then he opened Sir Marcus's letter, read it and to Thomas's surprise, threw it into the fire. The falconer waited, knowing that his future hung in the balance. He had of course not told all; and he was not sure how well he would be able to conceal certain other matters from his master.

At last Sir Robert looked at him and said: 'I fear the cruel slaughter of those hawks has upset my wife very much.'

Thomas nodded. 'There was retribution perhaps, in the killer's death. I hope that the new birds I have brought might serve to ease her distress a little.'

But Sir Robert was not listening to him. He looked out of the window and watched the treetops waving in the wind. 'Was your wife always honest and open-hearted with you, about everything?' he asked suddenly and turned to look Thomas in the eye.

A knot hardened in Thomas's stomach. Carefully, he answered: 'I believe she was, sir. Though I have no means by which to be certain.'

'Indeed,' Sir Robert answered. 'We have no line long enough to plumb the well of a woman's mind, once she chooses to conceal anything.'

Thomas was silent.

'My wife is changed, since I brought her home from London,' Sir Robert went on. 'By that,' he added quickly, 'I do not mean she - I mean she is still a true and devoted wife to me, in every way.'

He fumbled for the words. 'But she is - I might say, distant. She rides the new Barbary mare I have given her every day and does not wish for company.'

'Sir Robert,' Thomas began, equally hesitant, 'I believe I must take some blame in the matter. I failed to protect her ladyship as well as I might, during our stay in Sir Marcus's house - she was frightened by intruders, and then there was the killing of the birds...' he trailed off, for Sir Robert had held up a hand.

'I have read Sir Marcus's words. And I know you well enough, I think. I will not condemn you.'

Thomas waited while Sir Robert drifted into another reverie. When he came out of it and saw the falconer still standing before him, he asked: 'You still wish to be falconer here?'

'With all my heart, sir. This is my home.'

'Good.' Sir Robert sighed. 'I had feared you had it in mind to ask leave to quit my service.'

'No, sir,' Thomas replied in surprise. 'Nothing was further from my mind.'

'There is naught on your conscience, then?'

Thomas met the other man's eyes, but could discern nothing.

'I could not truthfully say that, sir,' he answered. There was a moment's silence, before Sir Robert seemed to recover a little of his old brusqueness.

'I must let you return to your work. The hawks have been fed and exercised, but no man here has your way with them.' He paused, and added: 'Your daughter is well, and has made herself useful. She is a good-natured child.'

'I thank you, sir,' Thomas answered, with relief. It seemed that his life might go on, as before. Though, watching his master's thoughtful face, he still felt a stab of unease. But when Sir Robert spoke again, it was of a different matter entirely.

'My son has been in trouble at Oxford,' he said. 'I can't get to the nub of it, but I fear that if he

continues to behave like a wild rake, he shall be sent down.'

Thomas frowned, remembering John Pollard and his tormented love for the selfish William Vicary. How many more of this family's secrets were known to him, and not to his master? He was suddenly weary. It must have showed on his features, for Sir Robert said suddenly: 'You have had a long ride. Go to your daughter now. The steward has sent her home to light a fire. I believe I saw smoke from your cottage.'

Thomas nodded gratefully and bowed, but Sir Robert had turned away from him, and was staring out of the window. Without further word he left the room and went out of the house.

After his meeting with Sir Robert, Eleanor's simple welcome was a blessing and a joy. She hugged him, tears starting from her eyes, as they stood inside the doorway of the cottage.

'I thought the very worst,' she said. 'No one knew what was become of you. Promise me you will not stay away so long again.'

'I promise,' he answered.

'But you are hurt!' she exclaimed, looking up at his face.

'I'm sorry I forgot your gift from London,' he said. She shook her head to dismiss it, her arms about him still, then looked up when he added: 'But I stopped in Reading this morning and remembered.'

He drew a fine handkerchief of white lawn from one pocket and from another, a cascade of coloured ribbons: red, yellow and blue. She took them and smiled wide with delight, then held them to the light to examine them closely. He watched her and thought that in the two weeks he had been absent she seemed to have grown up alarmingly. He closed the door and took off his jerkin and boots, grateful for the warmth of the fire she had made. She moved happily about the cottage getting a supper ready, while he found a candle and lit it. Suddenly she was still, aware of his eyes upon her.

'You are very like your mother now,' he said.

Looking at the floor, she asked: 'Will you ever marry again?'

He looked surprised. 'I had not thought of it.'

'If you did, I would try to be a good daughter to... whoever she was.'

He thought for a moment. 'There is no one at present,' he said. She nodded and returned to setting the table.

Early in the morning, after a night of uninterrupted sleep, he went to the falcon's mews. The birds had been fed and watered, but badly needed exercise. They roused on their perches; some of the older birds peered sharply at him as if in recognition. The little merlin, bright-eyed, regarded him critically. Now he had the two great gyrfalcons to train as well; he had placed them outside on the grass, tethered to hooped perches away from the other birds. There was much to be done, but he would set to with a will.

Just then, one of the gardener's lads came over from the house with a message: while Lady Margaret was eager to see the new birds, this morning she would ride on the Downs with her merlin. Thomas should take a horse from the stable and meet her on Greenhill Down in two hours.

He watched the boy go, then turned thoughtfully to his work. The instruction was half-expected; and the meeting had naught to do with hawking. He feared it, yet looked forward to it with an equal measure of excitement. Whatever its outcome, he would at least be able to bring her the news he had kept hidden from everyone else. What might follow from it, he did not know.

He worked in the mews for more than an hour, then hooded the little merlin and took it out on his gauntlet. He took no bird for himself; he would exercise them later. Long nights without sleep stretched ahead, if he was to sit up weathering the new hawks. There would be little time for anything but work, from now on. The notion comforted him; he wanted to busy himself.

After looking in at the cottage to tell Eleanor, he went directly to the stable, saddled a horse and rode out with the merlin on his hand. The day was chilly but fair, and he was soon trotting uphill with the breeze in his face. One thought had begun to dominate all others; he would be alone with Lady Margaret again. He brushed it aside; the news he had to tell her, would soon render all his romantic notions obsolete.

Then he saw her riding towards him, and his heart leapt.

She reined the spirited Barbary mare up close to him and smiled slightly when he offered her the merlin. She brought out her embroidered gauntlet, slipped it on and took the bird on her fist.

'I have not meant to neglect her,' she said, stroking the feathers with a gloved finger. 'I wanted to wait until you returned. I knew you would do so, whatever others have said.' She paused. 'I fear to ask what you have learned.'

He nodded. 'I'm uncertain where to begin.'

'Your face!' she cried, seeing the livid scar on his cheek. He shrugged; he was not seeking her sympathy.

'Let us ride slowly,' she said, and turned the mare's head. Urging his own horse forward, he

moved alongside her. After they had walked the mounts in silence for some minutes, she said: 'Sir Robert told me all that you told him, and I have guessed more. I must reward you - you have suffered much for my sake.'

He frowned. 'I ask no reward - and besides, I-'

She cut him short. 'You have had nothing from me. What passed between us in that house must be deemed a dream, nothing more. Is that clear?'

He was silent. Finally, he said: 'You know I will never speak of it, to anyone. But it was no dream and can never be such to me.'

Her face softened, and he saw now the sadness she bore.

'I should leave here,' he said, suddenly dispirited. 'Take my daughter and seek a new position far away. I have wronged you, and your husband.'

'No!' she was stern with him. 'If wrong was done, it was at my bidding. You did not pursue me.'

He gave a tight smile. 'I needed little persuasion.'

But her mind was drifting elsewhere. Seeing her agitation, he was reminded with a jolt, not entirely pleasant, of his conversation on Bankside only three days ago, with Susanna Lynch. The resemblance between the two women was even more striking now.

She turned to him. 'My daughter is to be betrothed, to Sir William Stanton's son. It makes me feel old, very suddenly.'

He started, then realized she was speaking of Anne. She watched his reaction, and said quietly:

'You had better tell me of your discoveries.'

They rode for an hour across the Downs, then turned back. She allowed him to talk, asking very few questions. If she was shocked to learn that her bastard daughter was a wealthy bawd and a celebrated whore, the plaything of some unnamed Lord, she took the news calmly enough. The riddle of her brother's death was solved at least, she said, and perhaps that ought to be the end of it.

Then, not without anxiety, he told her the last part: of how Susanna longed to see her, if only the once.

To his dismay, she reined in the mare and turned fiercely upon him. 'How dared you suggest that! You had no right!'

'I know it,' he answered. 'Yet if you had looked upon her, as I did-'

'And seen what?' she demanded. 'Is her resemblance to me so striking, that it turned your

head?'

'Perhaps it did. She is said to be the most beautiful woman in London. A dark lady, yet very like you.'

Her eyes dropped. 'She is dark-skinned.'

'She whitens it, yet she cannot hide her eyes. They are black as a falcon's.'

She was silent. Carefully, he said: 'She told me she would like to know more, about her father.'

After a moment she clicked her tongue to the mare, which stepped forward. Thomas rode beside her.

'That was the strength of your brother's grip on you, was it not?' he dared to ask now. 'If your husband learned of the child it would be bad enough, but that her father was a Catholic - worse, a Spaniard...' he trailed off, for she had turned sharply.

'Who told you this?' she asked.

'No one told me with certainty,' he answered. 'Yet that is the rumour I have gleaned.'

She shook her head then, and tears started from her eyes. She reined in again and held out the merlin to him.

'Take her from me,' she said.

He took the bird on to his gauntlet, speaking soothingly to it until it settled. Lady Margaret pulled out a kerchief. Now she put her face into it and wept, while he watched helplessly.

'So that is what they thought,' she said finally, and wiped her eyes. 'Well - he was no Spaniard, and certainly no priest.' she laughed, not unpleasantly. 'He was a heathen.'

'Not an ape, then,' he blurted, and bit his lip in regret.

But she was not angry; she almost smiled. 'Why, I believe you have been talking again with old Granny Hall.'

He nodded. 'She is superstitious.'

'So was Cusebo,' she replied. 'He believed that if he died here in England, his soul would never be able to find its way home.'

Thomas stared uncomprehendingly. She lowered her eyes, then said: 'I will trust you with this. You and you alone.'

He could help his curiosity no longer. 'Is he dead?' he asked.

She nodded. 'He is certain to be, by now. He was sold into slavery, by Nathaniel.'

He waited patiently, until she told him all.

'He was a man of the Americas. Tall and brown-skinned, with shining black hair, rare as a

forest God. A native of Florida, captured off a French ship and brought to London by Captain Hawkins. He caused quite a stir at Deptford, I believe. That was in 1565; I was a girl of seventeen.'

She paused. 'To many - to scoffing fools like Nathaniel - he was no more than an ape, for he knew no English, and his language was strange to our ears. Yet my father saw beyond such ignorance. Nor would he permit him to be shown at the fairgrounds like a beast. He took him into our home, and treated him as an honoured guest, and taught him to speak. He wanted to learn all he could of his people and his country. And when the Indian understood, he returned our affection. His name was Cusebo. He was brave, and wise, and gentle, once we had learned to converse with him. And he was a prince, too, among his own people. It was my privilege to know him.'

When she had finished, Thomas said: 'You must have loved him deeply, to risk all that you did.'

She smiled. 'I was fearless, then. And once I had grown accustomed to him I saw he was a man, in some ways no different from any other. I thought not of the consequences.'

She touched her heels to the mare's flanks and rode away towards the edge of the Downs. Trotting more slowly behind with the merlin, Thomas followed. After a mile or two she fell back and waited for him to catch up. They rode in silence; Thomas found that he had no words left.

But within sight of Petbury she reined in and sat looking down at the smoke blowing from the chimneys.

'It would be a terrible risk,' she said.

He started and turned. 'You would meet her?'

'I do not know. Can I dare to trust someone like that?'

He shrugged. 'She is ruthless and clever for one so young - strange, too. I suppose it would be dangerous to trust her.'

The merlin mantled on his fist. 'She is hungry,' Lady Margaret said. 'We have talked, and not let her hunt.'

Thomas stroked the little falcon until she calmed, and said: 'I will feed her now, and exercise her later.'

She was thoughtful again. 'I will ponder this matter,' she said at last.

He nodded. 'Whatever you ask of me, I will do it.' He paused. 'I am after all, your devoted servant.'

She looked closely at him, but there was no sarcasm in his expression. He smiled. 'You have not yet made acquaintance of the new gyrfalcons.'

'Sir Robert is eager for a hawking party soon,' she said. 'It would cheer him.' She lowered her eyes. 'He and I are...' she trailed off. 'I must go to him now.'

Thomas nodded; his heart was heavy. The secret would always be with them, but the closeness they had shared for that one night was past; it would but fade to a memory. Touching his cap, he kneed his horse forward, but she spurred her mare away at once and outran him, breaking into a canter, downhill to Petbury.

The merlin swayed and gripped his hand tightly, as he followed at a calmer pace. At least, he felt the burden of his dearly-bought intelligence had been lifted from him.

CHAPTER 19

A week later, on a clear, cold night bright with stars and a halfmoon, Thomas was at the falcon's mews while the rest of Petbury slept. He had sat up almost every night since his return with the new haggards, the wild-caught gyrfalcons that he was training. It was essential to tire them, to keep them awake until they grew accustomed to him, and to their new life. It would be weeks before they were ready to soar like the other tame hawks, even on the long line called a 'creance', but he had great hopes for both birds. Sir Robert and Lady Margaret had started to go hawking again, and a large party of guests was expected in mid-November. Sir William and Lady Stanton would be among them, partly as a celebration of the betrothal of their son to Anne Vicary. Sir Robert had promised fine hawking, if the weather proved fair.

Thomas had given the tercel a scrap of meat from a basin, and was picking out another for the female, when he heard a sound from the beech woods beyond his cottage. He stood up, walked to the side of the lean-to and peered towards the tree-line, but could see nothing. Still, he was on the alert. The old gardener, who knew every hill and tussock within five miles of the manor, had claimed two days ago that he had seen human tracks in the wood. Nobody would have paid his story much attention, save that some feathers were found near the poultry pens. Poachers were suspected, and Sir Robert had ordered his men to be vigilant.

As Thomas was on the point of turning away, the sound came again. It sounded like the crack of a dead branch. Taking a thumb-stick from the lean-to, he started to walk across the stretch of long grass towards the trees. He had not taken his lantern and was thinking of returning for it when there was a crash, ahead and to his right. He froze, just as a large stag sprang from the trees, its antlers brushing the lower branches. Only yards away, it veered sharply and bounded full-tilt towards the open country beyond. Its hoof-beats thudded off into the distance, and startled night-birds screeched in the wood.

Thomas laughed a short laugh to himself, relaxed and turned to walk back; too late, he heard the rapid swish of a man's boots coming towards him through the grass. He spun around as a dark figure hurled itself against him, knocking him flat. As he lay winded, the man bent over him with something like a snarl and stretched his hand out. Thomas felt the sharp, ice-cold point of a dagger pressed against his throat.

'Wouldn't I do it?' the man spat, in a hoarse voice. His breath stank of strong drink. 'Move one muscle, you whoreson javel, and you'll find out!'

He knew the voice, before he made out the twisted features above the unkempt beard: John
Lynch.

'I've watched you,' Lynch breathed. 'Like a father to your falcons, eh? How'd it be if I broke a few of their necks? Would that move you?'

Thomas kept rigid, breathing steadily. His right hand was some inches from the thumb-stick, which lay beside him in the grass.

Lynch saw it, grabbed it and threw it away.

'You've played me for a fool from the beginning. No longer, falconer! You'll learn your lesson - late, but not too late. First tell me what I want to know, and you'll live a while yet.'

Thomas saw him more clearly now. This was not the John Lynch who had faced him triumphantly across the table on Bankside, backed by his ruffians; nor even the John Lynch he had followed along Houndsditch, furtive and alone. The man who glared down at him now was lean, grim and red-eyed from lack of sleep, his face dirty, his clothes stinking of stale sweat. How long he had been living here in the woods, it was hard to say; but he had not the air of a vagrom man who has merely taken to the road again. He looked every inch a fugitive, driven to desperation. More than that, there was a wild look in his eye that signalled he was capable of anything.

'Ask what you will,' Thomas said. 'You have the advantage.'

Lynch coughed suddenly. When he spoke, he was almost wheezing. But never did he relax the pressure of the poniard against his victim's skin.

'I know that well enough,' he breathed. 'Your part is to tell me where she is - now!'

Thomas felt his pulse quicken. As calmly as he was able, he asked: 'Where who is?'

'Don't try that, falconer,' Lynch whispered, and jabbed the poniard into his flesh, causing a sharp pain. 'Don't spare it a thought, lest I stick you like a pig. I have followed her all the way from Southwark, and I know she is here somewhere!'

Thomas had thought instinctively that the man meant Lady Margaret; now, it seemed that was not the case. His eyes must have flickered with relief, for Lynch bent his face closer and smiled. It was a wild, humourless smile, and it reminded Thomas suddenly of Laughing Morgan. Lynch looked perilously close to insanity.

'Mistook me, eh? No matter, for you shall tell all.' He raised his head a fraction, looked towards the cottage and asked: 'Your girl in bed asleep, is she? The pretty little wanton with the ribboned hair?'

Thomas clenched both fists involuntarily. He could feel a trickle of blood now, running down his neck.

'I watched her today, from the woods,' Lynch said, looking him in the eye and savouring the effect. 'She is a little young, but not too young to be pinked by a ruffler. It's only right, that we follow the custom of the vagrom folk.'

'You touch her and I'll kill you,' Thomas said softly. But Lynch laughed, and his eyes gleamed.

'Now we come to it, falconer,' he said, nodding his head up and down quickly. 'Now you're ready to trade.'

'If you speak of your - of Mistress Lynch,' Thomas said, 'I know nothing of her whereabouts.'

Lynch's face twisted savagely. 'Liar! She is here - I know it!'

'Then she has not made herself known to me,' Thomas answered through his teeth.

'You take her part, too,' Lynch cried. 'At every turn, she thwarts me - I should have strangled her when she was a mewling babe, like I was paid to do!'

He was almost frothing with impotent rage. Quickly now, Thomas sought to divert him.

'I know the country - I could find out where she is,' he said.

But Lynch would not listen. With another jab of the dagger he spluttered: 'Get up before I spike your eyes!'

Thomas got to his feet, his clothes soaking wet from the long grass. All the while Lynch kept the dagger tight against his throat.

'Now walk to your stinking hut,' Lynch ordered. 'And if you try to shout, I'll slit your pipe.'

Heavily, Thomas began to walk the twenty yards towards his cottage. Beyond, the stables and outbuildings were barely visible; no lights showed. Help was not nearly close enough. They rounded the comer of the falcon's mews, Lynch beside him, gripping his arm. His other hand held the poniard. Thomas's thoughts raced wildly, but one resolve had formed itself: whatever it took, he was not about to let Lynch get close to Eleanor.

As they passed the open front of the lean-to the hawks shifted restlessly on their perches. The new falcons were particularly nervous; the tercel lifted its wings, darting its head forward.

Thomas stopped suddenly, so that Lynch collided with him. But the ruffian stepped back at once, without letting the poniard slip. 'Move on!' he snapped.

'The birds are uneasy,' Thomas said. 'They might call out.'

At once Lynch pushed his face close to Thomas's ear, and said: 'I warned you about playing me for a fool, falconer. I know they will not make a sound!'

An inner voice spoke to Thomas: now, and only now. He raised his boot and stamped it down hard upon Lynch's foot.

He gave a strangled cry. For a second the dagger-point dropped away, which was time enough. Thomas dug his right elbow into Lynch's stomach and as the man doubled over, half turned and brought his fist up under his jaw.

Lynch gave a gurgling scream as his teeth were smacked together, slicing through the end of his tongue. He staggered back, the tongue hanging half-off and blood running from his mouth. At once Thomas lifted his head and shouted in the direction of the house.

'Alarm! Intruders! Here!'

But Lynch was not done. Wild with rage and pain, he raised the poniard and flew at Thomas, as from the distant kennels dogs started barking. Thomas tensed in a half-crouch and grabbed hold of the arm as it came down. Then, surprised at the strength of the man who was a head shorter than he was, he found himself grappling for his life. Close to the lean-to they fought, locked together like two drunken men. Lynch's face was a livid mask dripping with blood as he kicked, punched and gouged at Thomas, oblivious now to everything else except the urge to maim and kill. He was a beast at bay, and if he had lost he would make someone pay before he fell. Thomas using all his strength, managed to wrest the dagger from Lynch's grasp but the ruffler's other hand closed about his throat, and his fingers sank into the flesh like claws.

Thomas struck wildly at the man's face, his neck, his chest, but still Lynch held on. With his other hand he grabbed Thomas by the wrist and tried to force him downwards. The next moment they had overbalanced and fallen to the ground. Lynch was on his knees, but still he tightened his grip on Thomas's throat.

A dizziness was coming over Thomas. Fighting for breath, he took hold of Lynch's wrist and tried to pull it away, but the man held on like a crab. The two traded punches again and again, feebly now, both of them growing weak. Bloodied and bruised, they fought on, even as the dogs barked and a shout came from the house, followed by others.

Desperately, Thomas brought his head forward and banged Lynch across the bridge of his nose. The man's breath flew out with a hiss, his eyes rolled and his head went back, yet somehow he still kept a hold on Thomas's throat. But he had let his other hand fly loose and

seizing his chance Thomas gripped it and bent it backwards with all the strength he could muster.

There was a sickening crunch of bone. Lynch screamed and let go, whereupon Thomas

raised his fist and smashed it into the centre of his face. Now the man fell back, and Thomas struggled to his feet. From a distance he saw lanterns and running figures. Ahead streaked the dogs, barking loudly. Thomas reeled, trying to clear his head, and banged against the corner post of the lean-to. From behind him, came a whirling of wings.

He turned with sudden alarm, thinking of the birds. As he did so, he sensed somehow that his opponent had got to his feet and turned back to see that Lynch had picked up the dagger. His face a red mask, the ruffler raised his good hand and took a step forward, stumbling against one of the hoop perches. There came a loud creak, but Lynch ignored it and advanced on Thomas, who backed away, keeping his eyes on his opponent.

There was a splitting of saplings, a whirring of wings and a flurry of feathers, as the huge female gyrfalcon that had pulled free of its perch, flew at Lynch's face.

Lynch screamed, dropped the dagger and put his hands to the striking bird, which jabbed its beak into his eyes with the force of a hatchet. One claw raked open his cheek, the other tore a gash from forehead to neck. Thomas stood, dazed and breathless, unable to do more than watch as with one hand Lynch tried feebly to pull the hawk away. Then at last it let him go and, beating its wings furiously, flew up and hovered above him.

The next second, the hunting dogs bounded up baying for blood; Lynch turned and ran, howling in terror.

He ran towards the trees, while the men of Petbury came running up, lanterns swinging. James and another groom, followed by the fat beekeeper, came to a halt beside Thomas and stared in horror.

Lynch did not even reach the tree-line before the hunting dogs, with Nathaniel Pickering's three half-wild hounds in the forefront, overtook him. Snarling and slavering, the pack bore him to the ground and leapt upon him, fighting with each other to reach his throat. The watchers heard his screams and saw his arms flail about briefly, then he was hidden beneath the mass of heaving animals.

Recovering their wits, the men hurried forward to drag the dogs off, but already it was too late; from the torn body on the grass, there was neither movement nor sound.

In the faint glimmer of dawn, Sir Robert Vicary was woken from his bed by an apologetic but anxious steward. Pulling on boots and cloak, he left the house and followed Martin out to the field beyond the stables where a silent group of men stood, some holding lanterns. To one side, Thomas the falconer was sitting on the grass holding a blood-stained rag to his face. As Sir Robert approached, the men parted to reveal a body covered with a horse-blanket. He

ordered the blanket drawn back, and after some hesitation the men obeyed.

There was a moment's silence before the older groom ventured: 'Nobody knows who he was, sir. A thief, a vagrom man mayhap; not of this parish.'

Martin murmured to Sir Robert that with a face so badly disfigured, it was unlikely he could ever be identified. Sir Robert turned to Thomas, who was getting slowly to his feet, his face covered with bruises. The knight gazed at him.

'Can you walk a little way with me?' he asked.

Thomas nodded. Sir Robert issued curt instructions to his men, then stalked away, followed by his steward and his falconer. They did not speak until they had rounded the wall into the stable-yard. Then Sir Robert stopped and said: 'I will send for a surgeon to treat your wounds.'

'Your pardon, Sir Robert,' Thomas answered, 'but I can tend to myself. I am not mortally hurt.'

Sir Robert looked keenly at him. 'What happened?'

Thomas summarized the events briefly, omitting those facts known only to himself. When he had finished, Sir Robert turned to Martin and said quietly: 'I would not like my wife to know of this matter. She is nervous as a colt of late - ever since the visit to London. It was unwise of me to let her go.'

Martin was frowning. 'The coroner,' he began, but Sir Robert broke in.

'There will be no inquest. The man was a vagabond and a poacher, and his death was an accident. I will speak privately with Sir William Stanton.'

The pedantic steward was still uneasy. He coughed politely and asked: 'What arrangements then should I make, sir? I mean, with regard to the burial.'

Irritably, Sir Robert answered: 'Dig a pit in the woods, for all I care. Use your wits.'

Turning to Thomas, he said: 'The hawks, I entrust to your care as always. They will take a deal of settling down, after this.'

'I will see to it,' Thomas said, with a bitter taste in his mouth. A man had been killed – a wicked man, perhaps, but Sir Robert's thoughts were only of his hunting party.

But when the knight spoke, it was as if he wished to explain himself. 'I want things ordered,' he said. 'I want things to be - as they were!'

There was a plaintive note in his voice. He looked towards the house, and muttered: 'All was well here, until the day Nathaniel Pickering came to stay. He said for a month - which became a year; now he remains for eternity.'

Without looking at either of them, he walked away.

Not wishing to alarm Eleanor, Thomas did not return immediately to the cottage. Instead, as a pale sun rose above the rooftops, he washed in the horse-trough. James, about his morning duties, emerged from the stable and saw him. At once he took Thomas to the harness room and bade him sit while he found some ointment.

'It's a family remedy,' James told him. 'I've salved many a good horse with it.' He opened the jar, stuck his finger in it and pulled out a lump of grease. Thomas winced as he dabbed it unceremoniously on to his face.

'Pity Jane Bull's not here,' the groom said with a sly grin. 'You'll have to make do with me, though I'm not so handsome.'

When he had finished he straightened, surveying his work with a critical eye. Thomas thanked him and rose stiffly.

'You're lucky to be alive, Thomas,' James said. 'A man like that would have slit your throat, robbed you and Lord knows what else.' He paused. 'For a falconer, you have an odd way of attracting trouble.'

'Not any longer, if I can help it,' Thomas told him. 'I'll keep to my hawks. They're less cruel than men.'

He went back to the cottage to find Eleanor already at the door, looking out for him. When she saw his face her hand flew to her mouth, but he gave a tired smile and stayed her.

'I am not badly hurt,' he told her. 'I will be myself in a few days.'

'There's a boy here,' she said, flustered. 'He's been waiting to speak with you.'

As he entered, a young man in a fustian coat got up from the table, fumbling with his cap. When he saw Thomas, his eyes widened.

'Good morning to you, master,' he said nervously. 'Are you Thomas Finbow, the falconer?'

Thomas nodded. Behind him Eleanor shut the door and said: 'I gave him a drink and a bit of bread. He's walked all the way from Wantage.'

'Indeed?' Thomas looked in surprise at the boy, who said:

'I'm the post-boy from the Ram's Head Inn, sir. I've been sent with a private message. From a lady.'

Thomas moved towards the table and gestured to the boy to sit. But he remained on his feet and pulled a handkerchief from his pocket.

'I was told to see you and no one else,' the boy said. 'The lady said I was to give you this.'

He opened the handkerchief, but Thomas already knew what it contained. With a sigh, he

sat down and watched while the boy unwrapped a large ring with ornate straplines of red-enamelled gold, and a tiny carved figure at its centre.

CHAPTER 20

It was not until the next day that he was able to speak to Lady Margaret. She sent word that she would go riding alone, taking her merlin. Thomas was not asked to accompany her; she would come by the mews and collect the bird herself.

When she rode up and saw him waiting, she guessed that he had something to impart. He held the mare's rein while she dismounted. Formally she gave him good morning, then raised a plucked eyebrow. When he told her that Susanna Lynch was lodged at the Inn in Wantage, she was aghast.

Almost furtively, she glanced towards the house, then to the cottage-door. At that moment Eleanor came out to empty a basin of slops. Seeing Lady Margaret, she blushed and curtsied low, and hurried back inside.

'Does anyone else know of this?' Lady Margaret asked.

'Eleanor saw the token,' he replied. 'But she will keep the matter secret, as I asked.'

She turned about and took a pace, putting a gloved hand to her brow. 'If I refuse to meet her, she may expose me,' she said, as if in argument with herself. 'She will want to do me harm.'

He felt pity for her, as he had done that day when they stood in the room overlooking the river in Sir Marcus Brooke's house. He wanted to be of help, yet the decision was hers.

'If you meet her,' he began. Lady Margaret looked up sharply.

'If you meet her, I believe she would take every care,' he finished, aware how lame the words sounded. 'She has reasons of her own for discretion.'

'No doubt,' Lady Margaret replied, then asked: 'Do you have the token?'

Thomas nodded and took it from his pocket. When he placed it in her hand she drew breath quickly.

'Did she say how she came by this?'

He shook his head. 'Do you recognize it, my lady?'

She gazed long at it. 'It was my mother's. My father gave it to her, when they were very young. It was believed lost.'

Then she faced him and said: 'It seems that I have little choice. But then perhaps in some way, neither does she.'

The following afternoon, Lady Margaret and her falconer rode westwards on to the hills, in full view of the house. Three miles away on Lamboum Down, in full view of no one but a few sheep, they turned north-east and rode briskly towards the village of Wantage.

At the Ram's Head Inn, they clattered under an arch into the cobbled yard and drew rein. At once an old ostler appeared to take the horses. The man touched his cap respectfully when he saw Lady Margaret and nodded to Thomas, whom he recognized. Thomas dismounted, helped Lady Margaret down from the saddle, then dropped a shilling into the man's palm. His jaw dropped.

Drawing him aside, Thomas asked: 'Who is it you see, Henry?'

Henry's forehead creased. 'Why, I see you, Thomas.'

'I rode to Wantage to find the blacksmith,' Thomas told him, 'because my horse lost a shoe on the Downs. You saw me, but did you see anyone else?'

He fixed Henry with a piercing look. Slowly, the furrows faded from Henry's brow.

'I don't believe I did,' he answered.

'Good,' Thomas said. 'And when I leave this evening - alone again - there's another shilling for you.'

Unable to stop himself, Henry rubbed his hands. As Lady Margaret disappeared inside the inn without word or sign, he bowed so low that his forehead almost brushed his apron.

'By the Lord, Thomas,' he mumbled when they were alone, 'this day has been powerful strange. There's another fine lady lodged within, has give me sixpence to say she never had no visitors.'

Thomas said nothing, but turned and led his horse out of the inn-yard. If Henry noticed that the animal did not appear to have lost a shoe, he put the thought away at once and hurried about his business.

Thomas returned two hours later as the light was fading, and lanterns showed at the windows of the Ram's Head. He led his horse into the yard and gave the rein a turn-about a hitching- post, then glanced about. There was no sign of Lady Margaret.

At that moment Henry appeared in the stable doorway. Thomas walked to him and asked if anyone within had ordered a horse to be ready. Henry shook his head.

'There's no one come out since you been gone,' he said.

Thomas frowned. She had said she would be waiting, but perhaps the assignation had lasted longer than intended. He found an upturned ale-barrel in a corner of the yard and sat down to wait.

A quarter-hour passed, then a half. It was pitch dark now, and he grew uneasy. Getting to his feet, he walked into the stable and found Henry. The old man nodded in answer to his

question, came to the doorway with him and pointed to an upstairs window, where a light showed.

'The best chamber. Last door on the right, as you climb.' Thomas walked to the entrance and ascended the stairs. There was no one about. A few moments later he stood outside the door and hesitated. Then he heard voices raised within.

Feeling like an intruder, he started to move away, but the voices grew louder. Two women in the room were shouting at one another; and there was no mistaking who they were.

He bit his lip, raised a hand to knock, then stopped himself. Whatever was going on within, he was not likely to be welcomed. Then someone cried out, and he thought only of Lady Margaret's safety. Grasping the latch, he opened the door and took a step inside.

They stood close together in the candlelight, beside a table in the window. Lady Margaret looked distraught, her face wet with tears; Susanna Lynch, flushed with anger, was facing her. Seeing the two of them like this, Thomas stopped in spite of himself and stared. They were unmistakably now, mother and daughter. Lady Margaret, in a plum-coloured dress trimmed with lace, was breathing heavily, one hand outstretched as if to call back something she had uttered in haste. The other, in a sober dress of dark blue and a starched ruff, looked remarkably unlike a Bankside bawd, and very like a lady.

But to his dismay Thomas saw that she had struck Lady Margaret; her hand hung trembling in the air still, as if by its own will it might strike again.

Instead, a sob broke from Susanna's throat. The next moment the two women had thrown themselves into each other's arms and were clasped in a tight embrace, weeping like sisters.

Thomas turned and went out at once, closing the door behind him.

Some minutes later, when Lady Margaret emerged from the inn in her hood and cloak, Thomas had the Barbary mare saddled and ready. Without a word she let him help her mount, then the two of them rode out of the yard, through the village and away towards the Downs.

She did not speak for some miles, until they had turned eastwards towards Petbury. Then she slowed her horse to a walk and allowed him to ride alongside her. When she began to talk, calmly and unhurriedly, he breathed a sigh of relief.

'It is done,' she said. 'She and I will not see each other again. We knew a moment's closeness, and that is all we may expect. We are so far apart in every way; we must live as strangers.'

He said nothing.

'She was done a terrible wrong, of which only you are aware,' she went on, adding: 'And I am forever in your debt.'

They rode a little way in silence before she continued: 'She asked that I thank you. She wishes to reward you in some way, if it were possible.'

He looked nonplussed. 'I have no wish to go to London, my lady. Ever again.'

She managed a smile. 'I expected that was the case.'

After another moment, she said: 'She has torn up Nathaniel's debts, and offered to restore my father's house to me.'

He was surprised. 'That was a kindly act.'

'I suggested a better plan,' Lady Margaret answered. 'That she should keep the house and live in it herself.'

He frowned, but she went on: 'She wishes to be free of the bonds she owes to a certain Lord and live as her own woman. She will have no master, she swears, ever again.'

'She is courageous,' he said.

'Indeed,' Lady Margaret nodded. 'She has much of her father in her.'

Then there was a catch in her throat, as she said: 'The bravest deed of all, is that she has promised to play her part, for the remainder of her life. To the world, that devil John Lynch was her father. She will stay a ruffler's child.'

Both of them were silent, as they rode slowly down towards the lights of Petbury.

On a crisp November day, as fallen leaves crackled under-hoof with frost, the hawking party moved out from Petbury and ascended the Downs. The gentry rode in a cheerful, talkative group, their breath hanging like steam in the air. Sir Robert and Lady Margaret, each with a bird on the fist, rode together with their daughter Anne, and young Daniel Stanton. It cheered the grooms, the men with the setter dogs, and Thomas the falconer, to see all of them in good spirits.

Winter was fast approaching. Mary Stuart, Queen of Scots, had been found guilty of treason at Fotheringay Castle; the danger to Queen Elizabeth was revealed. Though the times were as uncertain as any, the future that lay ahead might now be brighter. People of all stations had hopes of a better harvest next year.

Thomas had brought the gyrfalcons, though they were scarcely broken from the lure. During a lull in the hunting Sir Robert rode over with his fine hawk and reined his horse in beside Thomas. Slipping the hood over the bird's head, he handed him down.

'Put Glory on the cadge,' he said. 'I've a mind to try the new female.'

Thomas hesitated. 'She is wild yet, sir, and may carry or even fly off.'

'Still, I will try her,' Sir Robert answered, and held out his gauntleted hand.

Thomas took the bird from the pegged frame on to his own gauntlet, stroking its feathers and murmuring quietly. As he lifted it towards Sir Robert, it shifted nervously.

'I am uneasy to let you take her, sir,' Thomas said. But impatiently, Sir Robert replied: 'On my own head be it.'

Thomas held his gauntlet out, loosened the jesses and coaxed the unwilling falcon on to Sir Robert's wrist. As the great bird gripped tightly, Sir Robert pulled off its hood and held it up proudly.

'See, Sir William,' he called to his guest. 'My new prize. What shall I name her?'

Sir William and the rest of the party had ridden over. As they reined in the bird mantled angrily, stretching its huge wings out.

'You have not hold of the jesses, Sir Robert,' Thomas warned. Startled, the knight gripped the leather thongs, but was too late. Some distance away, the dogs had flushed out a pheasant. With a flurry of wings, the bird raced from its covert and flew aloft.

In an instant, the female gyrfalcon had launched itself free of Sir Robert's hand and soared high above the heads of the startled group. As they watched with a mixture of anxiety and admiration, it sped after the pheasant, overtook it, turned about, stooped swiftly through the air and caught it at full tilt. There was a wild fluttering and a shower of feathers, and the luckless game-bird dropped like a stone.

The watchers raised a shout, but Thomas was silent; he knew what was about to happen. Instead of returning to its master, the great bird hovered, then shot high into the air, until it was but a speck, barely visible against a sapphire blue sky.

'By the Lord, but she's magnificent,' Sir Robert said. 'I am mightily afraid to lose her.'

Lady Margaret had ridden up and sat silently on her horse. All eyes were on the gyrfalcon. Its partner the tercel sat docilely on the cadge, indifferent to events.

'She will come down,' Lady Margaret said. 'They pair for life, do they not?'

'Indeed,' Sir Robert answered. Then he gave a joyful shout and pointed as the bird began to drop, ready to stoop at some other game. The watchers breathed sighs of relief; it would return sooner or later.

'You have done well with the two of them, in such a short time,' Sir Robert said to Thomas, then spurred his horse forward, following the dogs. The remainder of the party wheeled their mounts and rode after him.

Lady Margaret held back until they had gone and looked down at Thomas. Their eyes met, but there was only a shyness in hers as she returned his gaze. Sharply she turned, shook the mare's reins and cantered away from him across the grass.

Printed in Great Britain
by Amazon